# Dangerous Dream

by
**Felice Buckvar**

# Royal Fireworks Press

Unionville, New York

Toronto, Ontario

For Manny Gutman and Rose Cohen, who survived concentration camps when they were in their teens, and the late Israel Peled, a member of the Palestinian Brigade of the British Eighth Army. They helped me write this book by sharing their personal histories of World War II and postwar Europe with me.

Royal Fireworks Press
First Avenue, PO Box 399
Unionville, NY 10988-0399
(914) 726-4444
FAX: (914) 726-3824
email: rfpress@frontiernet.net

Royal Fireworks Press
78 Biddeford Avenue
Downsview, Ontario
M3H 1K4 Canada
FAX: (416) 633-3010

ISBN: 0-88092-277-X

Printed in the United States of America using vegetable-based inks on acid-free, recycled paper by the Royal Fireworks Printing Co. of Unionville, New York.

"...a Gestapo member was apprehended in a Jewish DP camp near Bremen, and an SS man was caught living with a Jewish woman in another camp.

"I know a small inn near Merano, in the Italian Tyrol, and another place near the Reschenpass between Austria and Italy, where illegal Nazi transports and illegal Jewish transports sometimes spent the night without knowing of each other's presence."

Simon Wiesenthal
*The Murderers Among Us*

# Preface

Autumn, 1945. The deadliest war in the history of the world has ended with Germany's surrender in May and Japan's some months later. The Allies—Americans, British, French, and Russians—now govern Germany, Austria, and Italy, mostly in separate zones of occupation.

Europe is teeming with refugees. Many are civilians forced by the Nazis into slave labor. Some are soldiers returning from service. Displaced Persons camps have been set up as temporary shelters for the refugees on their way home.

The Jews of Europe had been a special target of Adolph Hitler, the dictator of Nazi Germany. They had been herded into concentration camps for slave labor and eventual murder. A small number had hidden with kind neighbors or in convents. Others changed their identities and lived in the general population or banded with secret groups fighting the Germans. Now many found themselves the sole survivors of their families, their homes destroyed or taken over by neighbors who refused to relinquish them.

Most of this "Saved Remnant," as they called themselves, live with one hope: to settle in Palestine, their ancient homeland, the Biblical Land of Israel. They vow to live in the D.P. camps for years, if necessary. In the meantime, they prepare themselves for Aliyah, permanent resettlement in Palestine, by learning farming methods for the desert country and practicing reading and speaking Hebrew. They call their study groups "kibbutzim," named after the collective farms worked and run by Jews already living in Palestine.

Getting to Palestine is not easy. Although America's President Truman supports the return of the displaced Jews to Palestine, the British, who govern the country, will allow in only a fraction of the Jews yearning to live there. Some Jews will try to get there by any means possible, alone or through underground Jewish organizations, but their way is dangerous, and any misstep might return them to the devastated, dismal continent that is Europe in 1945.

## CHAPTER ONE

# A Dream Comes True

"There's a new list."

The news flashed through the waiting room of the hospital like a ray of sunshine through dark clouds. Everyone waited for the lists of survivors, hoping to find the names of loved ones separated through war and disaster and flung to every miserable corner of Europe.

I heard the news just before taking some information from a man the Military Police had brought in. He had been near the entrance to our displaced persons camp, asking about getting some medication for a burn on his arm, and the M.P.s had shown him where to go. As a helper in the infirmary, I had to take his name and complaint and bring it to the nurses. Sometimes, I held a baby or watched a child when her mother was being examined. Often, I just ran from one person to the other as a shout or a groan summoned me.

Of course, in normal times, a thirteen-year-old wouldn't be doing this work, but what were normal times? Did anyone even remember them?

The man was sitting with his head bent over his arm, which I could see was red and yellow with burns and blisters in a regular rectangular pattern—no doubt, a self-inflicted wound. The injury was on the exact spot where numbers had been tattooed by the Nazis in charge of concentration camps, so I guessed that the man, like many of the Jews here in Landsberg, had survived one of the larger death or labor camps. My heart went out to him, for he was one of us, one of the Saved Remnant.

When he looked up from his arm, two piercing blue eyes met mine. Then he glanced away quickly, his face twisted in pain.

"Let me see your arm," I told him, but he sat there without moving until I put out my hand to bring the injury closer to me. As I studied the red, raw skin, he breathed noisily, as though with difficulty. *Poor man,* I thought, *to have caused himself so much pain to remove the tattoo he had been branded with.*

"The doctor will have something for the pain, I'm sure," I said. Standing poised, ready to begin filling out his information sheet with his name and address, I was distracted by a familiar voice.

"Hella! Did you hear about the list?"

My dearest friend, Margot, was approaching, her dark eyes shining with the news.

"Yes. Look for my father's name for me, will you?" I asked, for he was the only one out of all my family who might still be alive.

Months ago, right after the war had ended, Margot and I had searched for him in Berlin, where I came from, but our house was in ruins and no one admitted knowing my father or any of my family. Still, I thought of him almost every moment of consciousness, and in my daydreams he was alive, and we would find each other one day soon.

I reminded Margot of his name, "Hans Wilhelm Weiss. M.D.," I added.

"The name. What name did you say?" the man with the burned arm said hoarsely in German.

I myself usually spoke Yiddish, slipping from Yiddish to German without any conscious thought.

"The name?" he asked again.

2

For a moment, I didn't know what he was asking me.

"Your father's name?" he whispered, his voice shaking.

The way he asked me started my heart pounding. "Dr. Hans Wilhelm Weiss from Berlin." Every word I said was a prayer, for who knew when this man saw my father last and what he would tell me?

"Dr. Hans Weiss of Berlin," he repeated, his eyes widening, his mouth trembling. "My God!"

"What is it?"

"Ruth! You must be Ruth."

My ears filled with the drumbeat of my heart. "I'm Hella. Ruth was my older sister." Memories of Ruth rushed into my mind, together with the sounds of a harp. She had been a brilliant player, a child prodigy who, in normal times, would have enjoyed a career in music, for she won the praise of the master musicians she played for, Mama told me. I remember her endless hours of practice. Worried that she was always going to be too short, she used to try to stretch her legs until they throbbed with pain. I would help by holding down her ankles.

When the Nazis started rounding up Jews, my mother hid her with a German family, as she did me, but Ruth was soon discovered. The rest of her story was a nightmare familiar to every Jew in Landsberg, a nightmare we survivors endured. My darling sister, who I could never think of without hearing music as delicate as crystals of fresh snow, was killed when she was fourteen. A former teacher at our elementary school I met at the temporary D.P. camp at Saalfelden had seen her clubbed to death.

Now my voice was unsteady as I asked this strange man, "You knew Ruth?"

Instead of answering me directly, he asked, with voice quivering, "Is she—?"

I knew what he was asking. I named the concentration camp where she had been killed. "Treblinka."

"Your mother?"

Another camp. "Sobibor. She died of typhus."

*How odd,* I thought, *the way he asked questions a few syllables at a time, as though to say more would be to open floodgates which could not be closed against streaming memories.*

"You knew them?"

Solemnly, he nodded. Then he covered his face with his hands.

He knew them. He knew them well enough to mourn their deaths. My own eyes swam as I watched him.

*At the least, he would be a link to a past shattered so long ago, I barely recalled it. Perhaps he could even lead me to my father.* Catching my breath, then exhaling it, my heart beating almost painfully, I asked, "You knew my family in Berlin?"

About to reply, he stopped suddenly, glancing about and wetting his lips. No one was in hearing distance.

"When did you last see your father?" he asked.

*My father?* That was so long ago, almost beyond memory, for what I recalled was probably told to me by my mother and then the Burgers....

"Ten years ago—in 1935," I answered. "Why do you ask?" As I questioned him, I felt a layer of sweat form above my upper lip. "Have you seen him?"

4

Instead of replying to my question, he murmured, "You were a baby then."

"I was three. Please. Have you seen him?"

He burst out in gasps, as if he, too, could barely contain his emotion. "I know all this, Hella. I don't want to shock you." His eyes fluttered away, like a restless bird unable to hold still, then they returned to my face. "Don't you recognize me?"

I didn't, but I waited eagerly for him to say that he was a neighbor, a friend of the family's, or better yet, a relative, a cousin of my parents, perhaps.

Holding out his bony hands and enfolding mine in them, he drew me closer. "Hella, you have given me new life, my dear Hella."

*He knows me,* I thought. *He knows me well, although I can't recall...* "Yes?"

"Hella Weiss, I am your father."

His words rang in my ears like separate notes of music. I decided I must have daydreamed what I thought he had said. "What?"

"I am your father."

A roaring filled my ears, a weakness hit me in the knees. I always knew this moment would come, but I was sure I would be prepared with a rumor, a name on a list, an arranged meeting. The shock was too much, and for a moment, all was blackness and silence.

When I recovered, I was sitting next to him on the plain wooden bench. I had pictured this for so long. My daydreams about it were as natural to me as breathing, yet I'd never imagined how my emotions would overwhelm me. As I sat there shaking uncontrollably, my father put out a hand to steady me, touching me as though I were delicate glass that might break in his fingers.

I felt his sadness like a weight. *What he must have gone through to be unable now to embrace me freely,* I thought. Trying to bring him closer, I put my arm around his neck. Although he sat straight and stiff, he was shivering. Burying my head against his shirt, I hoped that his smell, perhaps, would evoke a memory of him. But, no, I could remember only a few things about him—or was I told about them by Ruth or my mother, and had I created my memory from theirs?

All my daydreams of him were based on hope and some half-recalled photographs—a stocky, smiling young man on the day he received his medical degree, a young father holding his first child on a pony, then at a park with an infant, me, and a toddler, Ruth.

I could hardly recall his features.

When I lifted my head, Sarah, one of the volunteer nurses, was standing before us. "What's this?" she asked in her brusque tone, the sides of her brown eyes crinkling into a mosaic. She, like Margot and most of the others, had survived the concentration camps alone and now waited with only one goal—to get to Palestine, the ancient Eretz Yisroel of the Bible.

My heart leaped as I told her, "A miracle, Sarah. This is my father, Dr. Weiss."

"Your father?" she exclaimed.

"Yes." I laughed gleefully at her expression, as she was staring open-mouthed, first at him, then at me.

Of course, it was a miracle to find any relative, let alone a parent. And my being in the hospital as a volunteer was because of my father. That was only a small part of the

6

miracle, for I wanted to pursue the same career that had been so abruptly interrupted for him.

I knew my ambition might have seemed more like one of those intricate daydreams with which I occupied my mind, as weavers and knitters keep their fingers busy creating beautiful designs. I had no real schooling to speak of, but from the moment my mother had taught me to read, I loved reading, and now I was devouring every book on medicine I could get my hands on. Besides, no matter how my friends teased me about daydreaming, I believed that my imagination helped me during those endless hours of hiding in the Burgers' apartment.

Then, later, on the farm where Maria Burger left me, how else could I have played my role so convincingly? I thoroughly imagined myself one of Hitler's loyal little girls, so that I could gather fresh eggs for the German soldiers, curtsying for them and answering their questions in character. Daydreams kept me going when all else led to despair.

Now as Sarah stood staring at my father, I studied him, too. His eyes were bright, intelligent, alive with questions and observations as they darted here and there. In one moment, they brushed my face, then peered over my shoulders and to the sides, then to Sarah's face before returning to me. His nose was sharp and mine flatter and rounder; I took after Mama and her family. They were Poles, and they looked Slavic.

My father did have light hair, like me, and he was tall and thin, while I was thin and still growing.

His dress white shirt was worn almost to tatters, the long sleeves rolled up past his elbows, and although his slacks were equally thinned and shiny with use, his clothes were not grimy, nor were they as shapeless as some I'd seen.

As Sarah and I looked at him, lines of worry creased his forehead.

He shook his head. "I am still dizzy with shock. You must forgive me if I forget my manners."

"Of course," Sarah murmured.

He took his eyes off us to glance around. Then he returned his gaze to us, leaning towards Sarah. "Listen. I am engaged in secret work for our people. You must keep this a secret. You must not say who I am. Do you understand?"

"Of course," I answered, my heart filling with pride. Whatever had happened to him, he was still a leader, as I always knew he would be.

Her face flushed with emotion, Sarah reassured him, "I understand, Doctor." Suddenly she opened her arms to encompass us. "God bless you both," she exclaimed.

Grimacing in pain, he held out his arm to her. "Do you have sulfa ointment here? That's what I need. That and a clean dressing."

"Yes, Dr. Weiss. We have sulfa," she answered him in Yiddish.

My father and I naturally fell into using German, our native language and the language we had spoken most often at home, but Sarah tried to avoid speaking in the tongue of her enemies.

"It shouldn't be too long until Dr. Muchnick sees you," she murmured with a glance at the other waiting patients. Gesturing to one of the seats, she added, "You should sit there and wait."

I stood to lead him as Sarah moved on to another new patient. His reactions were slow, I noticed, for he didn't move at all until I had gestured that I was going to bring

8

him to another seat. Limping, he followed me, tightly clutching a worn brown leather satchel in his hand. As we waited, I wrote his name on a paper together with a few words about his injury, struck, at that moment, by how like my daydreams reality had become for me. In my daydreams, I often found my father ill and in need of my help. And I always rescued him....

"Are there proper doctors here?" he asked me in German.

"We have wonderful doctors here. Our own people."

There was still so much I wanted to tell him. How I was at the hospital because of his example. How proud I was of him, and how that pride had always helped me. As his daughter, I had a special obligation to be brave, to assist others, to achieve all I could. Hadn't Mama always taught us that? Glowing with contentment, I realized I would have plenty of time to tell him everything.

My father sat in a heavy mahogany chair next to a Lithuanian whose name I had taken earlier. In this waiting room the furnishings, salvaged from homes and offices and schoolrooms, were as oddly matched as the people. The chair the Lithuanian sat on was of a crude light wood, possibly a teacher's chair once.

My father watched me and tried to smile, but between his pain and God knows what memories, the smile collapsed before it was fully formed, and I feared he might begin weeping from emotion. How my heart went out to him!

"What happened after they arrested you?" I asked. When he didn't answer, I told him what I knew. "Mama said you spoke up against Hitler from the very beginning, and the special police came to the house to arrest you. You were in Spandau prison at first, then Sachsenhausen, and then you were sent east. From that time, all she heard were rumors. What happened?"

9

Shaking his head, he waved his hand as though erasing my question from the air. "Some other time," he murmured.

I knew so many others like him who couldn't speak of the past, who kept their memories tightly shut away, for that was the only way they could live with them.

I wouldn't torment him with questions. Eventually, I'd find out everything. Instead, I volunteered my own history. "Mama took me to her friend, Maria Burger, the pharmacist, you know?" It occurred to me that he might not have known Herman and Maria Burger, but then I recalled that, of course, he knew them. I was too excited to think clearly.

"'Be strong,' Mama told me before she left me. 'Survive for me, my darling Hella. For me, you will be strong, remember!' They hid me until Herman was arrested in the winter of 1943," I told my father.

⌛    ⌛    ⌛

Emotion tightened my throat, as I pictured round, little Herman and the schoolbooks he found for me so I could learn mathematics and science, and the ribbons he bought for my hair.

"Why do you waste our money on foolishness?" Maria had chastised him.

We had no word or warning that Herman would be arrested. One evening, he simply didn't come home. Late that night, Maria decided to seek a man she knew who worked with Herman.

Returning to the apartment in the early hours of the morning, she closed the door quietly, her mouth formed an "O," and she began moaning almost silently. As she sobbed in strange, quiet gasps her fingers pulled at her hair, usually neatly pinned, until it fell in disarray.

10

I came close to comfort her, but she pushed me away. Her eyes widened as she stared at me, as though she had suddenly discovered me there.

"They took him. The Gestapo took him. It should have been you!" She spat the words at me as her arm shot up.

Before I knew what she was doing, my cheek stung with the unexpected slap. Again, she raised her hand, but this time, I escaped. She chased me and grabbed me by the arm, pulling me to the door.

"Go! Go!" she whispered hysterically. "Get out of here!"

*Where would I go? Who would help me? Within minutes, I would be arrested and sent east for slave labor.*

"No, please!" I begged her.

She hit me again and again in eerie silence, for if someone heard and reported us, we could both be deported. Finally, her arm tiring, she ceased beating me. "Tomorrow," she whispered. "Tomorrow you go!"

I gasped, "The farm. Herman said 'the farm.'"

He had often told us if anything happened to put us in danger, and he was not around, Maria should take me to a farm near Wittenberg where they had gone for vacation several times. The farmer was grateful to Maria for some medicine she had once brought for him. Maria was supposed to tell them I was an orphaned relative she could no longer care for.

When I mentioned the farm, Maria groaned and held her head in her hands. Why, I didn't know, for I no longer understood this woman I had thought was a second mother to me.

She gestured to me in disgust to leave her alone, but I dared to remind her, "For my mother's sake, bring me to the farm."

11

I knew there were other ways she could get rid of me. She wouldn't be punished if she killed me, saying she caught me robbing her apartment or that I was trying to get her to protect me. Only for keeping me safe was she in danger herself. With her eyes wild, her hair unkempt, her cheeks burning as she sat on the floor rocking back and forth and banging her fist against her forehead, she looked capable of anything.

After a moment, she arose, stumbling to the kitchen to gulp down some pills, which seemed to quiet her. Then she went to her bedroom and fell on her bed. In seconds, she was asleep.

I stayed awake all night in my dark corner, paralyzed with fear. *What was Maria planning to do with me?* A thousand times that night, I persuaded myself to run away and take my chances, but a thousand and one times I decided to trust Maria.

She awakened in the morning, whimpering like an injured dog. I kept as far out of her path as I could, and the only words she barked at me were, "You stay here."

Again, I waited with fear twisting in my stomach and pounding in my head, for Maria would probably have chosen to return with the Gestapo, if she would not risk her own life for having harbored me for so long.

She returned late, driving up to the apartment house in a car she sometimes borrowed. Recently, she and Herman rarely used the car, for gas was rationed and cost more than they could afford.

"You're leaving," she announced at once. "Get your things. One suitcase."

Before we left, she tied a ribbon with a religious cross hanging from it around my neck, then pulled a scarf over my hair to shade my face. "Speak to no one," she told me, "or I shall throw you out of the car before we reach the farm."

Walking out first with my suitcase, she led me to the car. Luckily, none of the neighbors was around.

Once we were out of Berlin, she spoke again, telling me what to say if the farmer asked about my family. I was to say that we were Catholic. Next, Maria made me recite prayers and practice crossing myself. She described how I was to take communion. "And don't act wise or sassy. If you speak out of turn, you'll get us both hanged!" she warned me.

When we had been driving a couple of hours, an air raid forced us to stop and turn off our headlights while bombs burst in what seemed a circle around us.

Since it was the middle of the night by the time we reached the farm, Maria had to awaken the farmer's wife. The woman recognized Maria, then looked me over with a critical eye as Maria told her about me. Or at least, about "me, her 'niece,' Hilda Schultz."

"She will have to do outside work and stay in the barn, unless she knows something good. Can she sew or bake good?"

Maria was quick to shake her head. "No, she has no special skills."

The farmer's wife echoed Maria's low assessment of me and sneered, "You think a city girl can find the barn?"

"Yes," I answered—humbly, I thought. But Maria looked annoyed. I realized I had answered too quickly, with too much confidence. "I-I think so."

"Then go," the farmer's wife directed me. "Kiss your aunt goodbye."

The kiss was as brief and as cold as hail.

13

"Obey your elders!" Maria warned me.

"Here." The farmer's wife sliced a piece of bread from a loaf and slid it across the long wooden table towards me.

Thanking her, I grabbed it. Both women seemed to be waiting for me to go, and so, too frightened to ask directions, I stumbled out of the house and into the darkness. While dogs I couldn't see barked ferociously at me, I finally found the barn. Opening the door took all my strength. I'd never been in a barn before, and the smells, the dung underfoot, the frightening movements and noises of the animals I awakened made me wonder if it all was worth it. Should I have given myself up in Berlin?

Somehow, I found a ladder that went up to a loft that was at least dry and not covered with droppings. I sank into an exhausted sleep that ended with the first of the nightmares that I would have for the next twenty-seven months as Hilda Schultz, a girl who acted little smarter and was no cleaner nor better-fed than the animals she cared for.

⧗　⧗　⧗

Now my father grabbed his wrist and moaned with pain.

"The doctor will be with you soon," I told him.

Meanwhile, a woman with a baby in her arms was standing near the door, looking about for assistance. Ordinarily, I would be helping her, and I felt torn between my duty to my job and my responsibility for my father.

"Do you mind if I take the information from that woman? After you see the doctor, I can take off and get you settled. I'll find you good accommodations...."

"No!" The idea seemed to startle him. Glancing suspiciously at the Lithuanian next to him, he asked in a sharp voice, "Do you speak German?"

14

Surprised, the man jumped away from him, indicating by a shake of his head and hands that he didn't understand the language.

Turning back to me, my father murmured, "I cannot stay here, Hella. I told you, I have important work to do."

My spirits soared, as I was certain of the important work he did, for he was extraordinary, wasn't he? He may have looked like the others—weary, depressed, in worn, almost threadbare clothing, but he was someone special. I immediately assumed the respectful tone of my mother when she spoke of her husband.

"You help Jews get to Palestine. Yes?" I guessed breathlessly.

Revealing heavy, yellowish teeth, unlike mine in size and texture, he almost smiled. "Clever girl," he said, his eyes widening in appreciation, I was sure, of my understanding.

Swelling with pride at the unexpected compliment, I became bolder. "You're with B'richa, aren't you?" I asked, naming a well-known underground organization.

Without answering, he pursed his lips, but his bright eyes shone with the little guessing game we were playing, and he nodded ever so slightly.

Yes, I had discovered his role so quickly! He was one of the heroes who came to Landsberg, a station along the way to our ancient homeland. He was helping Jews return to their Holy Land in spite of the orders of Palestine's British rulers who refused to let in all the Jews who yearned to live there. How brave Father must be, how knowledgeable and capable!

As eagerly as though I were offering him something tangible, I shared the latest news with him. "Only a few days ago a man came from Palestine to speak to us. Ben

15

Gurion was his name. He spoke in the sports hall." I was so excited that I was rambling, but my father listened to me with interest.

"What I'm doing is dangerous," he murmured when I was finished.

"I know. The British would put you in prison...."

"That's right. They're searching relentlessly for me, all the time." Leaning even closer, he said in a low voice, "That's precisely why you must not tell anyone else about me."

I thought of my friends. I had pictured their excitement when I told them my thrilling news. How disappointing now not to say anything!

"Why did you injure your arm?" I blurted out.

For a moment, his eyes darted away from mine. When they returned to my face, they were steady again. "It was identification. The British..."

"Hella!" Sarah's voice rang out, making me jump.

She was standing near the entrance next to a small woman bent over in pain. The woman with the baby I'd thought of helping moments before was now nowhere in sight.

"Excuse me," she added for my father's sake.

He raised his good hand to show he understood. Meanwhile, I glanced at the paper in my hand. "Is it all right to give your real name?"

He seemed to think about that for a moment. "I'm sure we can trust the good doctor. It's all right."

I thought I could read anxiety in his face. Although he accepted that Sarah needed me, we had only just met, a miracle in itself, and already I had to leave his side. "Don't worry," I told him. "You'll be all right here, and I'll be back in moments."

Again he dropped his voice, "Remember, don't tell anyone you met me."

If I could, I would have them announce our meeting over the loudspeakers. Let everyone rejoice with me and take heart themselves.

He seemed to be waiting for my promise.

"You can trust me," I reassured him. Shyly, I patted his shoulder, which seemed first to surprise and then please him. If I could, at that moment, I would have thrown my arms around him and held him as if I would never let go. And my words would ring in his ears: *Let me prove I'm worthy of you, Papa. Give me the chance to be brave and I will. With you, I will face any hardship, take any risk—for the rest of my life. I swear it!*

## CHAPTER TWO

# My Friends, My Father

The woman Sarah was hovering over was from Poland. Her face was as gray as the storm clouds outside, her body as frail as a sparrow's. Yet she was the type who would probably survive, for there was fire in her eyes, indicating a fierce will to live. The ones weighted down with guilt for having survived when all their family died, and the passive ones, were borne away like feathers on the wind.

I, too, knew despair, especially when I thought of Ruth being beaten, crying for mercy from the Nazi guards who killed her. Why did she die and not me? I had no answer, for she was the one with the God-given talent.

As I helped the woman to where my father was sitting, a thought started to flutter inside me. *Perhaps I had survived for that man, sitting and looking so lonely when I wasn't with him—and for our destiny to build a homeland together.*

"You are so like your father," my mother had told me again and again. "So like him..."

After taking the information from the Polish woman, I stood watching my father. How sad he looked. I knew he must be thinking of Ruth or my mother. Or his parents, my grandparents. Or...who knew who or what else?

"Hella!"

Again, I was being called. This time it was Margot, who was standing near the door to the hospital. With her were Olga and Esther, our other friends. Gesturing, I let them know I'd be with them soon.

I still had to bring the information I'd taken from the woman to the doctor. But, first, I stopped in front of my father. "Those are my friends at the doorway."

Without changing his expression, he turned to look in their direction.

"The dark-haired girl is Margot, my best friend in the world."

He nodded, but I could tell that his arm was still bothering him greatly. Thank God, the Lithuanian was next, and then my father would get some relief.

*How could I not tell Margot that I'd been reunited with my father?* I thought, as I made my way to her. We had met in a temporary D.P. camp months ago, right after her discharge from a hospital. She had been found with other starving survivors in a closed boxcar, the last place they had been left by the Nazi guards fleeing the approaching Allies.

She was only semi-conscious when an American soldier carried her to a truck that would take her to a hospital. When I first saw her, she was still little more than big eyes and a thin covering of skin over bones. Allowing no one close to her, she reminded me of a stray animal, snarling to keep everyone at bay. Assigned to the crudely boarded bunk right above me in our overcrowded camp, she made a terrible bunkmate.

For one thing, fearful of starving, she hoarded food, which attracted parades of roaches that used me and my bunk as their marching ground. In the middle of the night, Margot would shake and scream from nightmares, rousing me from the little rest I could manage myself.

One night, desperate for sleep, I tapped her on the foot while she was having a nightmare. Sitting up, she stared at me with wild eyes.

"You were screaming again."

"Leave me alone!" she shouted, slipping down from her bunk. As she ran from the room cursing, the groans of the girls she awakened followed her like waves breaking on a beach.

The next night, I awoke in the dark with an ache in my arm. Margot was standing over me, her bony finger pressed into my flesh.

"You have nightmares, too," she gloated.

Forgetting how light she was, I pushed her hand away too roughly. Compared to her, I was powerful.

When we were in line for food the next morning, she mocked me. "I don't know what you have to scream about," she said. "You had it easy."

*Easy? Fear had tainted every breath I took from the moment my mother left me with the Burgers. On the farm I did chores from before dawn to long after sundown with no one to speak to but the animals, for every other human being was an enemy. And she thought I had it easy.*

As time passed and we drew closer, I realized that next to the horrors she endured in three concentration camps, I did have it easy. After her last relative, an aunt, had died practically in her arms in Auschwitz, Margot had gotten sick and almost died, too. She never expected to live in freedom again.

Although I was almost fourteen months younger, I began feeling protective of her. Still, I was reluctant to take her with me to Berlin to search for my father. We would have to return to areas overrun with the Russians, foraging on our own for food and shelter. And it wasn't easy to go anywhere with Margot.

At first, she was afraid of anyone in a uniform. Then, after a few friendly encounters with American soldiers, she became dangerously bold, treating her life as though it were an annoying burden she would rather throw off than continue to carry. To hitch a ride, she would stand in the middle of the road until the jeep would stop. To eat, she would snitch food as soon as barter for it or wait in a line at some agency's kitchen. Only when she realized how she was endangering me, and then how much I needed her, did she change. Of course, she went everywhere with me, regardless of the danger.

Now when I reached her at the doorway, she took a close look at me and declared, "Something happened, didn't it?"

She caught me off-guard. Not knowing what to say, I ignored her all-too-accurate guess. "Did you meet one another at the office?" I asked as if nothing unusual had happened.

"We met there," contributed Olga, "but we had no luck with the new list."

"We're planning to eat early," Esther piped up. "We want to take a walk in town."

But Margot was not to be put off. "Either something happened since I saw you, Hella, or you're sick." She put out her small hand to touch my forehead. "You're hot. What's the matter?"

The concern in her voice and the fear in her eyes made my decision for me. I knew she could keep a confidence. "I'll tell you, Margot," I paused and looked reluctantly at the other two girls, "but I'm sorry, I can't tell anyone else."

Color blazed into Olga's cheeks. "No secrets!" she said, pushing a lock of auburn hair from her face. A beautiful girl with light skin and luxurious hair, she had hidden during the war in a Catholic orphanage where the nuns had fussed over the pretty child. They had known she was Jewish and had hoped that she would convert. But in the end, she left them to seek her family. As yet, she had found no one.

I took Margot by the arm, leading her further into the hospital.

"We won't be friends," Esther warned me in her sharp, no-nonsense manner.

I turned back to them. Esther had spent part of the war living with her Jewish uncle and his Christian wife. For a time, she and her uncle were allowed to live in a watchful, uneasy peace, but eventually they, too, were deported. Her uncle became ill and died almost immediately. Esther survived a half-dozen concentration camps, always hopeful that she would have a home to return to. When she sought her aunt after the war, she found her remarried, and wanting nothing to do with her former niece.

"I'm sorry," I told the two of them. "I promised not to tell a secret. Just to Margot," I ended weakly.

Esther looped her arm through Olga's. "Come on. Let's go." With her head of curly brown hair held high, she led her friend away.

Margot turned to me, her eyes wide with anticipation. But now I paused, stepping out of the way of a tall, thin woman carrying a wailing bundle. I waited until the woman had passed, then I began, my voice shaking. I knew what I had to tell Margot would change the two of us forever.

## CHAPTER THREE

# Good-bye, Best Friend

As I related what happened, the expression on Margot's face changed from interest, to surprise, to utter joy. Right there in the path of the front door, to the annoyance of a couple of Hungarian men trying to leave, she threw her arms around me and hugged me tightly in excitement.

I made her swear not to say anything to anyone else. "I shouldn't have told even you," I admitted.

"I won't tell anyone," she replied. "Can I see him?" she asked. "Please," she implored me.

I knew I should say no, but how could I? I thought of how little happiness she had known in her life, and my resolve melted like a spring snowfall.

"Come." With no intention of letting him see her, I led my friend to where she could observe him.

He was still waiting to be called by the doctor, and his eyes were downcast, as though he were deep in thought. "That's him," I whispered to Margot. "The one closest to the doctor's partition."

As she stepped closer to look, he lifted his eyes and turned to us.

Then she did something that was typically Margot. Without a glance back at me, she darted to him and was standing in front of him before I could even shout, *Don't!* There was nothing else for me to do but follow her.

"Please, sir," she was begging him in Yiddish. "Hella is my dearest friend. She is just like my sister. If you take her anywhere, take me, too. I won't be any trouble, I swear."

Surprised at her outburst, he turned to me with a questioning expression. "And why is she saying this to me?" he asked.

"It's true. She is like a sister to me," I told him. "We met at Ainring, and she traveled to Berlin with me, looking for you. When we couldn't find anyone who knew anything about where you were, we came here together. She has no one else but us."

"Us?"

"You and me."

"Next person," Dr. Muchnick called.

My father glanced towards the doctor and rose from his chair. "I cannot help you," he told Margot. "Perhaps Hella did not make it clear how important secrecy is for my mission. Did you?"

His tone towards me was sharp and it pierced me like a knife.

"I'm sorry." I almost called him "Papa." What a little fool I was becoming.

He made a slight bow to Margot. "I am sorry, my dear. If you are Hella's friend, you will say nothing to anyone. Please."

"Of course!" she cried.

When he had limped away into the examination area, Margot put her head on my shoulder. "I didn't mean to cause you trouble, Hella."

She seemed so forlorn that I hugged her out of pity. Of course, I forgave her.

Sinking into the chair my father had just sat in, I was aware that my whole body felt as though it were on fire. So much had happened so quickly, and now, when I looked up, Margot's dark eyes were searching my face. I read fear in her eyes, for she realized, as I did, that I couldn't continue to be a sister to her—and still do what my father demanded. As much as I loved Margot, I could only consider him and myself for the time being, or I'd lose him again.

"I know you meant no harm. Don't be concerned," I told her, the false reassurance tasting bitter in my mouth. "I'll see you later. Meanwhile, I want to wait for my—." Again, I almost said who he was out loud. "For him," I corrected myself.

"Yes, dear," she replied. In a moment, she was gone, blending into the crowd like a shadow.

I sat there, my senses aflame, unable to budge, my eyes on the door to the examination room.

When he didn't come out for awhile, I wondered if I had dreamed the reunion, after all. That happened regularly here, with visions of children and mothers and fathers and friends. Was it any wonder that we were crazy with heartbreak? But then he reappeared, his arm bandaged. *Papa! It is Papa!* I thought when I saw him. How I longed to call him that, if only to him, for it would be as soothing as the ointment on his arm, but it wasn't the right time or place. I sensed immediately that he was still angry with me.

"Margot left," I told him. "She meant no disrespect."

"Don't you realize you could endanger the lives of others?" he said, his voice a low growl. "Even my life."

"No," I cried, pressing my hands against my ears, for I could not bear to hear his words. "Margot won't say anything. I won't tell anyone else, I swear it."

He drew himself up to his full height, five foot ten or more, taller than most of the men in the camp. "We will be going through the Alps to Merano, and then south. But only if I can trust you. My mission is too important."

Tears stung my eyes. *How could he not trust me?*

He must have seen my hurt and taken pity on me, for he sighed, and in a softer voice he said, "Hella, my dear girl. Can you try to act older than your age? Can you try to think before you speak?"

"Yes, I understand," I cried. In my emotion I almost called him "Papa" again, but luckily I stopped myself in time. *How I would have loved to say that word, even to whisper it, but, of course, I mustn't,* I thought. *I must always think before speaking,* I admonished myself.

*The Alps. Italy. So much to plan and so little time.*

After looking around, he gestured for me to come closer to hear him. "There is something you have to do—and soon," he whispered. "Is it quieter here at night?"

I nodded.

Again he looked around. "I want to stay here tonight."

I didn't understand what he meant.

"I want to sleep here."

"Sleep here? You mean as a patient?" I asked.

"No, not as a patient. I want to find some spot where no one will bother me...."

"Why?" I blurted out.

Scowling, he echoed the word. "Why? Why must you ask why? Isn't it sufficient that I am your father and I said it?"

I didn't know how to answer him, for I wasn't the fool or the child he thought I was. It was simply my nature to want to understand everything I saw or heard.

Seeing my unhappy expression, he took pity on me.

"Hella, Hella," he said with a sigh. "My dear girl, I'm in pain, you see. I must do my job. Please understand."

"Of course." Again, I almost added, "Papa."

He winced as he touched me on the shoulder, but then he gazed into my eyes with love. "What a wonderful thing to find you. If only we could have hours, days, to become reacquainted. I know you have so much to tell me, but people depend on me. I mustn't fail them."

I sought the right answer and remembered my mother's words: "Your father is a great man. A prince among men."

"I am proud to be your daughter."

He squeezed my shoulder, and removed his hand. "You can help me. Is there anywhere I can hide in this place?"

I thought for a moment. There was a room used for storage. "I know a room, but it's locked."

"Can you get the keys?"

"Sarah has a set." I thought of the time Sarah was late and Doctor Muchnick had sent me to the administration building. Blushing and stammering, forgetting my English and lapsing into Yiddish, I asked Sergeant de Fillippi for the keys. He was the girls' idol, and for a week, my friends begged me to repeat the story.

"And there's an extra set of keys in the administration building," I told my father.

"Which would be easier to get?"

I answered without hesitation. "Sarah's."

His eyes narrowed. I felt he was studying me. "I want you to get them."

*Get them?* My mouth fell open. "Take them?"

27

His impatience flared. "Of course, take them!"

"I can't steal from Sarah!" I blurted out.

He drew back from me, his expression hardening in scorn.

Again I had disappointed him. *Oh, why did I have to say anything?* I wondered. *Why couldn't I simply do whatever he told me because he is my father, a brilliant doctor, a leader of our people? Why couldn't I keep my mouth shut and learn to follow?*

"Please, Papa. I didn't mean what I said. Of course, I'll..." I couldn't admit it was stealing, "...take the keys for you."

"I also need prescription blanks for the sanitarium in Italy to get us over the Austrian border. Where do they keep them?"

I told him where I had gotten papers for prescriptions for the doctors—on the shelf in the storage room, easily accessible to anyone hiding there. Now he seemed pleased with me, a smile almost flickering about his mouth.

"You will be a help to me, Hella," he murmured.

At the same moment, Sarah's voice rang out. "Hella, I need you."

She was standing in the midst of a family of Ukrainians, the mother holding a squalling infant, the father with two children in tow, one screaming in pain, the other shouting an explanation in an odd combination of phrases from many languages. They had created their own mob scene, and I knew Sarah needed another pair of hands while she led the howling toddler to the doctor.

I turned to my father questioningly. "Go," he said. "I'll find a seat. But don't forget..."

28

He didn't have to say any more. "I won't," I promised him, although I dreaded the thought of stealing from Sarah's pocketbook.

My opportunity came after I had managed to help get the Ukrainian family seated and take the necessary information from them.

An American soldier working on a jeep near the hospital had come in with a bloody surface injury to his foot, and the doctor had come out of his partitioned area to bandage the wound.

Acting as though I were still doing my job, I went behind the doctor's partition, opened the drawer where Sarah kept her pocketbook, and with my body hiding what I was doing from the patient awaiting the doctor's return, I opened the bag. With trembling fingers, I extracted the keys. Keeping them in my fist, clenched so hard that they made marks on my palm, I closed the pocketbook and the drawer and slipped outside.

As I passed the keys into my father's cool hand, he gestured me to come closer. I thought he might praise me for having done his bidding, but he only asked, "When do we sup?"

Dinner was served early. In fact, people were probably lining up for their food already.

"I want to leave this place while they are quieting down for the day, eat, then return and get a good sleep. We leave tomorrow at dawn."

"Tomorrow?" Of course, I should have realized it, but the idea took me by surprise.

He looked straight into my eyes. "Are you brave enough?"

I answered in a flush of emotion, "I'm brave enough!"

I asked permission from Sarah to leave earlier than usual, helped my father on with his raincoat, and led him out of the hospital along the path to the building where we got our meals. My friends and I usually carried our food to our room to eat.

Now the wind whipped against us as we made our way through the crowds to the dining hall, passing a group gathered around a Polish Jew selling winter hats—or rather, bartering them, as no one had money. Each of the hats was different. I recognized a Russian army hat and an American sports cap.

"You are a thief," the would-be buyer shouted, without real malice.

"And you will feel the wind between your ears all winter," answered the seller. The bartering, at its best, was entertainment.

I turned to my father with a smile at the banter, but he was scowling.

"This is how they fritter away their time?" he muttered.

The authorities, too, complained about the bartering, especially when it was between the people inside and the German townspeople outside the gate. But since the armed guards had been removed, no one could stop it. And the bartering did make the dullness of waiting in the camps a little more interesting. Still, I thrilled with the thought that my father was above such things.

I was still shy with him, but I said in admiration, "Not everyone's like you."

He looked pleased with my observation.

Feeling bolder, I continued, "Mama used to say you were a prince of a man. That's how she put it, and I thought you were a real prince when I was very little, like the princes in the fairy tales." When there was no reaction from him, I went on. "She said that's why they took you at the very beginning..."

We arrived at the place where lines had already formed to get dinner, and he kept his face turned away from the lines. Interrupting my reminiscences, he told me, "I don't want to stay here. Can you bring me my food?"

"Yes," I answered as some newcomers pushed their way towards the line, jostling us.

Jumping away, he grimaced. "Disgusting. Like Auschwitz."

Immediately, his comparison raised conflicting emotions in me. He hadn't told me yet where those numbers had been tattooed on his arm. Perhaps it was in that place of horror. I had heard enough about Auschwitz from Margot to know the difference between the discomforts we endured in the displaced persons camp and the absolute horror of a death camp.

"It's not bad here," I answered my father. "The food is good. General Eisenhower himself ordered better food for us. Now it's like a banquet."

I exaggerated, of course. I often found myself painting glorious pictures, as though I could change reality with my words.

He gave me an annoyed look. "I'll wait here for my banquet," he replied.

He was scoffing at me. Dejected, I walked away, thinking how I only wanted him to be proud of me and everything that I was a part of. I hurried to the line, determined to make up with efficiency for my childish speech.

There was still so much I wanted to ask him. So much I wanted to know. But he seemed reluctant to talk about the past.

*Many people here were like that, too,* I thought, as I took my place in the line.

Jack, the leader of our young people's "kibbutz"—named for the collective farms in Palestine—used to urge us to bury the past. "No one in my 'kibbutz' dwells on what happened to him. Why keep going over the same miserable history?"

I knew why our lives were pieces of puzzles in our hands. Beneath all our questions was only one: How did it come to pass that we were wrenched from our homes and families and hunted by an enemy who would kill us all? For that was the one bitter experience we all shared.

During the war, while I was feeding chickens, milking cows and cleaning stables, Jack was fighting against the Germans in the forests of the Soviet Union. The Russian partisans knew he was a Jew, but they accepted him, and he became as rough and fearless as any of them. The knife scar that ran on his dark skin from his right cheek to his mouth was a constant reminder of the struggle a German soldier had put up at close range before Jack killed him. He often touched it when he was emotional, and I once asked him why. "I can feel it throb," he said. "Like a heartbeat." I had thought it was more like a mark of courage, a medal that gave him the confidence so many of the girls found attractive. I was no exception.

*Even now,* I thought, warming to the thought of Jack, *he couldn't wait to begin his future in Palestine, could he?* Only the day before he and Norbert, his closest friend, left to make their way to Italy, and from there to Palestine, the exact journey we would be taking. Like us, they could be turned back at any step. We had often spoken about the heartbreak of being captured by the British and forced to turn around within sight of the Holy Land.

I could hear their farewells, "See you in Eretz Yisroel." Suddenly thrilling to the thought, I realized we might well meet somewhere along the way. Yes. We probably would meet, for it only took a day or two of delay for them—and what was a day or two when it came to travel?—and good luck for us.

Supper was a stew, mainly from vegetables, and lots of black bread, which I carried as carefully as if I were being tested by the way I carried dinner.

Before taking a bite, he examined the stew and the bread closely. Then, since he didn't want to go back to my room or mingle with the others, we ate outside standing up, his back to the crowds, his satchel on the ground between his feet.

He wrapped the bread we didn't finish, in a handkerchief he took from his satchel. On another equally ragged cloth he took from the bag, he wiped his fingers carefully.

"What time does the hospital get busy in the morning?" he asked when he was through.

"People start lining up before eight."

"We'll be gone by then," he muttered under his breath.

"Do we need anything special?" I asked him. "Warmer clothing?" He had mentioned the Alps.

Glancing around, he would not answer until a young woman had passed. "Bring as many of your things as you can carry without difficulty, but don't ask anyone for anything else. No one must know where we are going. No one! Promise me."

Out of his sight, I crossed my fingers, as I had learned from a girl who worked at the farm during harvest. "I promise," I lied, for I knew I could never leave Margot without telling her.

He gestured that I should put my empty bowl on the ground next to his. "Leave it," he said. "And let's go."

For a moment I hesitated, for I always brought back my dishes, but then I followed his example. I thought, *He makes his own rules, as he goes along, like all great men.*

As we started back to the hospital, I told him about Jack and Norbert. He nodded impatiently. Obviously, what others did was of little interest to him.

When we reached the hospital, he told me to look inside. "Tell me if I can get to the room undetected."

I opened the door. There was one person waiting, head down, near the doctor's partition. But no nurses or other personnel were in sight.

"I think it's safe," I told him.

"Come in and watch me. If anyone stops me, you come and correct me, as if I didn't know where to go."

"We'll meet at the side of the hospital at dawn," he murmured as he limped into the building. Then he stopped suddenly, turning to me. "Goodnight, my child."

How beautiful those words were. "Good night, Papa," I whispered back.

A warm hand patted my shoulder and his eyes embraced me with a father's love. For a moment, we stood basking in our good fortune.

Then he was limping to the room where he was going to sleep. When he was about to open the door with the key, Doctor Muchnick came out of his partition. My heart pounded with fear, but the doctor spoke to a man waiting there, then both of them disappeared behind the partition without a glance around. When I looked again at the storage room, the door was closed.

*Let him be well,* I prayed as I made my way back to my room. *Let him be safe.*

Later that evening, Margot and I left the camp to walk around the old town of Landsberg, standing much as it did hundreds of years ago. It was in a rural section, and although weapons had been manufactured in some of the buildings on the grounds of our D.P. camp, the town had never been bombed, nor was there fighting nearby. Margot and I had traveled to Berlin where almost every building had been blasted apart and stood as a useless, empty shell. Still, even in Landsberg, there were many signs of the German defeat: townspeople wheeling barrows of whatever firewood they could find before winter, soldiers stumbling through the town on their way to God knows where, and traders bartering anything they owned or could find in exchange for the American cigarettes which were far more valuable than German money. As we walked, I told Margot everything, unconsciously using the same words of warning that my father had used with me.

Then, feelings I had not sorted through until I heard myself express them surprised me as well as Margot. "He doesn't understand that I'm not a child anymore. I took care of myself during the war, without anyone's help."

There, that old bitterness had resurfaced. Even though I knew it was illogical, my anger always returned. I had been abandoned repeatedly, first by my father, then my mother, then by Maria.

We continued our walk in silence, but I was conscious of her labored breathing, from a heavy heart, I guessed.

35

Then came her accusation, spoken in a choked whisper, "What will happen is that you'll go and soon you'll forget about me."

"No!" I exclaimed. "Why do you think I would ever do that?"

"I know how it is. If you're lonely, you stay lonely. Anything in between only makes it worse when you're left alone again."

An idea occurred to me. "I tell you what. Let's think of each other every day at a certain time."

"What do you mean?" As she turned to look at me, her eyes widened.

"Every night, let's say at seven, we'll think of one another and think of telling each other what happened during the day."

She looked doubtful, but what else could I offer her?

"How will I know what time it is?"

"I know. Let's make it every night when the sun goes down, just before dark. How's that?"

"Yes," she said, slipping her arm through mine. "I'll probably be thinking of you anyway."

I could picture how it would be for her, and for the moment, I lost all taste for my adventure. "You know, I don't have to go with him. I can wait until we go together. Eventually, we'll get there."

She shook her head. "I'll meet you there. Don't wait for me." She stopped under a tree where a streetlight illuminated the colors of the falling wind-torn leaves, red and yellow, like the scarf hanging loosely down the front of her coat.

"You better put your scarf on," I warned her, knowing that even a breeze could make her sick. *Who will look after her when I'm gone?* I thought, as she covered her head.

She bent to pick up a perfect leaf at her feet.

"How beautiful," I exclaimed as she showed it to me.

She thrust it at me. She was always giving me the best of anything she had—the least worn clothing distributed by the relief organizations, the treats the American soldiers sometimes handed us. Now I took the hand that held the leaf, then threw my arms about her. *This is our good-bye,* I thought, *for when we go back to our room, I wouldn't be able to speak about my leaving.* The wind stirred the leaves around our feet, and as she shivered in my arms, I felt a drop of rain on my face.

"Come!" Pulling me back in the direction of the camp as droplets pelted us, she joked, "Tell your father to order better weather for tomorrow."

I couldn't answer. For the moment, I was breathless with an emotion I hadn't felt for months—pure, undiluted, unthinking fear.

## CHAPTER FOUR

# The Station

I said nothing to Margot about my fears, for I didn't want to burden her any more than I already had. She was going to be lonely without me, much more than I without her. I had my father now.

*Everything new is frightening,* I thought as we ran through the rain. When I fled the farm after hearing the Russian army was near, for days I was choked with fear. Of course, I welcomed the Allies, but I had heard news of the vengeful Russians, whose own people had been starved and slaughtered by the Germans, and I feared they would treat me as they treated the other Germans. Even half-starved, with only some eggs and some onions to last me until I reached the American troops, I could barely get down my food, for my throat had constricted with fear. Then I met Margot, and with new responsibility, my anxiety doubled until we finally were settled together in the displaced persons camp in Landsberg.

Now we returned to our room, which we shared with fifteen others, and to our beds with mattresses made of burlap bags filled with straw. The barracks were filled; too little space for too many people and not enough sinks or toilets or showers. The windows were so small it seemed as though the sunlight was rationed, but, after all, the camp was only a stopping-off place on our way to Palestine. Here, at least, were friends with whom to share our dreams.

"Do you want my red bag?" Margot asked me.

She had found a strange red carpet bag in a house requisitioned for us by an American soldier shortly after liberation. He had been so kind to us.

38

"Take whatever you want," the red-headed American had told us, even before he had chased away the German woman who lived there with her young son.

He wanted us to translate what he said into German. "Tell them not to come back for a week."

When I did not understand him, he spoke more slowly, "Not Monday, not Tuesday, not Wednesday. You understand?"

"Yes."

"And if you're still here, they have to stay away for another week. Tell them."

I translated his order. Cowering before the young conqueror, they left with many of their belongings in the suitcases they carried. I recalled Herman and his kindness to me, and I planned to use the house gently until Margot found photographs hidden behind a bookcase: a picture of a strutting Hitler, another of a man in an officer's uniform, no doubt the father of the house.

I broke the glass in the frames and ripped up the photos, hoping for the release that action sometimes brought, but anything that revived memories soon led to a sadness bordering on despair. As she sat silent, shriveled within herself, I asked Margot what the matter was, and she began the toneless recital I would hear again and again from her, starting with the march of the Jews through her town to the train depot. "The man who fixed our roof. The woman who sold us bread. Did they have to throw rocks at us?"

Now, months later, I reminded Margot, "I have my own valise," for I, too, had found useful things in the house, and the American soldier had prodded us to take whatever we liked.

I packed my few items of clothing, distributed to us by American agencies, then went to bathe. When I returned, Margot was sitting with Olga on Esther's bed, next to mine, watching for me while Esther braided Olga's long, thick auburn hair. When Esther turned to me, she raised a dark eyebrow in question to let me know that she had not forgotten what had happened earlier in the day. Behind her back, Margot playfully made a gesture of begging. I knew what she meant. Our friends loved apologies, and since I did not want to part from them in anger, I would have to act humble.

"Esther, Olga, I'm sorry about this afternoon. Please forgive me," I said.

Esther held her arms out, and I hugged her and then Olga.

"So what's your secret?" Olga asked even before she released me from our embrace.

"I promise you'll know at least part of it tomorrow. You'll see."

That seemed to satisfy them, and when they said good-night, I added, "I'm glad we're all friends again." Then I kissed them good-night, lingering longest with Margot who gave one soft sob that no one else saw or heard.

"Wake me in the morning," Margot whispered.

"I will," I told her.

Too excited to fall asleep immediately, I wove a drama in my mind. We were in Palestine, my father and I, but instead of his leading me, I was the one who taught him about farming. How patient I was as I showed him and the others how to plant. What a good example....

When I awoke it was dark, but a woman was winding her way from the bathroom to her bed. "What time is it? When will it be daybreak?"

"A good half-hour to dawn," she answered. "Go back to sleep."

That woke Margot. "Are you dressed yet?"

"Not yet." I jumped out of my bed into hers, but when my cheek touched her pillow, I felt the wetness. "Don't cry," I told her. Her answer was to hold me close and dampen my face with her tears.

The sky seemed to be getting lighter. "I have to go," I told her, drawing away from her as gently as I could.

When I returned from washing, she was dressed. On top of my suitcase, she had placed her favorite possession, a porcelain ballerina on a music box which, when wound, played "The Blue Danube" while the ballerina turned. A Romanian had it at the transient camp we went to after Berlin, though where he got it was anyone's guess. Margot was fascinated with it, for it brought back for her memories of a house in the country, a piano her mother played, and serene days in the long-ago past.

It had taken almost everything I had carried out of the German woman's house plus some of the things the Jewish agencies gave me to buy it from the Romanian, but in the end it was worth it. Surprising Margot with the gift was the happiest time in years, although there were days afterwards when I would have gladly wrung the ballerina's neck just to stop the interminable music.

Now Margot wanted me to take it back. "I couldn't," I told her.

"Please," she said. "I won't play it anyway until we're together again. I'd rather you kept it."

Opening my valise, I wrapped the music box safely in a blouse. "We'll listen to it in Palestine," I told Margot.

Olga sat up in bed. "Where are you going?"

41

Surprised, I blurted out, "I'm sorry, Olga. I can't tell you."

"Margot, too?" she asked.

"No, Margot isn't coming with me."

She seemed so surprised at that, she made me realize anew that I was deserting Margot, and I answered her more angrily than her question deserved. "I can't tell you anything else."

Her eyes narrowed as she looked at me, as though I were turning into a stranger right before her. I sat down on her bed next to her. "I'm sorry, Olga. I'm going where we'll all meet again." Quickly I kissed her cheek. "Tell Esther good-bye for me."

"Go with God," she whispered hoarsely.

Margot followed me out. Since it had rained at night, the air was crisp and clean, and I suddenly felt full of excitement with the adventure of my trip.

As we walked, I put an arm around Margot. "Don't tell anyone else, but soon we'll be in the Alps, then Merano, Italy, and then south to a port in Italy where we'll get on a boat to Palestine." I could picture it all like scenes from one of those plays Herman used to read to me. "I'll leave a message for you at the immigration centers in Palestine, so that when you arrive, the first thing you should do is go there. Wherever I am living, there will be a place for you."

She nodded, but I could tell that her thoughts were sad, probably on the past and other partings. She could never picture the future as vividly as I, nor as hopefully. She saw us tossed on a violent sea, our ship captured by the British while I felt the sunshine and the warmth of that magical, faraway place and happily daydreamed how we would work together there, satisfied in our labors.

As we approached the turn near the hospital, I stopped. "Go back, Margot." A last hug, tighter than usual. "I'll be waiting for you," I told her. Then she turned and was gone.

As I went on, my view of the side of the hospital still restricted, I wondered with a catch in my throat, *Would he be there?* I hadn't considered the possibility before, but he might well have decided that his mission would be safer without me. *Oh, no,* I thought, picking up speed as I made my way, although the suitcase I carried hit my leg with each step as I rushed. But when I turned and could see the side of the infirmary, there he was, sitting on a rock.

*I really was going to Eretz Yisroel with my father,* the thought surging through my body like a jolt of electricity. *I would run all the way, if it would get us there sooner!*

But as I came closer, I saw he was holding his arm and grimacing with the pain. My heart went out to him.

"It still hurts?" I asked.

Glancing up, he muttered, "I'll bear it." With some difficulty, he rose and lifted his bag from the ground. "Let's get started."

I smiled—for encouragement, at the pleasure of being with him, and with the excitement of beginning our journey —but he regarded me oddly, as though our business were too important for frivolity, and I felt foolish for having smiled.

*The Americans smiled a lot,* I thought as I began walking, recalling the people who worked for UNRRA, the United Nations Relief and Rehabilitation Administration, who ran our D.P. camp. *Even the American soldiers,* I mused, *and they walked differently, too. They walked easily, with a graceful swing that came from confidence and good food.*

"Did you take soap?" my father asked sharply, startling me out of my thoughts. Even with his limp, he walked more quickly than I did, and I had to scurry to keep up with him.

"Yes, I took three big pieces."

"Good." He was holding his arm again, and I assumed he wanted the soap to clean his arm, preventing further infection. "You're a good girl," he added. I almost smiled, then caught myself.

Not many people were out on the paths this early, just a few refugees and some American soldiers. I was hoping to get a chance to see Sergeant de Fillippi again, although what I would say to him, I didn't know. But he was not among the soldiers.

We went out of the gate from the camp into the streets of Landsberg. Our coming and going was unrestricted now, although at one time there were armed soldiers standing at the entrance. Now people complained that Germans from the town, even Nazi sympathizers, sneaked regularly into the camp for free food and whatever else they could get, but no one wanted to go back to the old way.

A milkman with a horse-drawn cart was making deliveries to the houses, which were all in a row, most of them built at the same time centuries before. In one of the doorways, an unkempt German soldier slept snoring, the empty sleeve of his uniform pinned above a missing elbow. Far beyond, the Alps loomed, like the backdrop for a play.

As we neared the railway station, the number of people on the street increased. One woman passed us, holding a sign with the picture and the name of her son. A family sat around a big pot waiting for the sticks beneath it to heat whatever was in it. Closer to the train, there were crowds, and with them, noise and foul smells. Looking disgusted, pressing a handkerchief to his nose, my father made his way towards the train, weaving and pushing through the groups of people, getting them to move out of his way. I was not as bold, and every few feet, he had to wait for me. Finally, he stopped. "You wait here," he told me. "I'll make the arrangements and return for you."

Trying to be helpful, I suggested, "You can leave your satchel with me," but he ignored my suggestion, and continued on, forging ahead in a straight line like the train we were hoping to board.

Putting my valise down, I stood where he left me, trying to follow his path with my eyes, when the sound of my name startled me.

"Hella! What are you doing here?"

Two friendly faces were only a few feet away. "Jack! Norbert!" I exclaimed. I was surprised to meet them so soon, for they did have a day's head start. *What luck!* I thought, beaming at them. Laughing with delight, we all hugged awkwardly. Of course, they were shocked to see me.

Jack, the shorter and huskier of the two, had curly brown hair, dark brown eyes and the confident, decisive manner of a born leader. No wonder my friends and I admired him so. Norbert, on the other hand, was angular in face, tall and thin and somewhat awkward in his ways. But he had a kind heart, and I could speak to him as a friend, without all the awkward stammers and blushes that punctuated my discussions with Jack.

Now Jack was explaining, "We're still waiting to get on the train. There are rumors it will be leaving this morning."

"What about you?" Norbert asked. "What are you doing here?"

For a moment, I hesitated, my father's warnings echoing in my ears. *But, of course, Jack and Norbert were part of the same secret group we were. In fact, once I got my father and them together, we might be able to travel together,* I thought with an excited thump of my heart.

"Are you alone?" Jack asked, looking around.

"No." They were both waiting for my explanation. Breathlessly, I began. "Yesterday, a wonderful thing happened to me," I began. They were both listening intently, and, in that second, it seemed that time hung suspended as they waited for me to continue. "I found my father."

"Oh, Hella!" Jack put an arm around my shoulder and squeezed it with emotion.

Norbert, too, took a step closer to me. "How did it happen?" he asked.

I told them how he came into the hospital—and why he had burned the numbers off his arm. "You see, he's working for B'richa, too," I whispered. "I'm on a mission with him."

"Then you may leave on the same boat as us," Norbert suggested. "Towards the middle of November."

"We're going by way of Merano, Italy," Jack said in a lowered voice.

"Merano, yes!" I blurted out, for I remembered my father's naming that town.

"We're meeting others at the Alpine Inn there before the Sabbath, we hope, and from there, we're going south to the coast." Gesturing impatiently at the crowds, he muttered, "That is, if we ever get out of here."

"Did you have breakfast, Hella?" Norbert asked.

I shook my head.

46

He took out a round cheese from the bag he was holding and carefully cut three chunks from it. We stood there eating the cheese as though we were back outside our barracks. When I finished, I saw my father searching for me in the crowds. I raised my hand and he spotted me. "There he is," I cried, pointing him out to my friends. Jack stepped forward eagerly to greet him, but as my father came limping closer and saw I was with the boys, he scowled with displeasure.

Certain that he would be happy to meet them as soon as he found out who they were, I greeted him with my introductions. "These boys are from my 'kibbutz' at the camp. Jack was our leader, and this is Norbert."

"I'm glad to meet you, sir. I hear we are headed for the same place."

For a moment he seemed confused, his eyes darting from Jack and Norbert to me and back again, his head twitching as though he were trying to rearrange his thoughts like the pictures in a kaleidoscope. Then he straightened up to his full height and nodded agreeably to the boys.

"It is a pleasure to meet you," he told them in his formal manner, lapsing again into German. "I don't know what Hella told you, but I have an important agenda to follow, and we must try to leave as soon as we can. Say good-bye to your friends," he told me. "I am sure you understand," he said to the boys.

Before they could reply, he took me by the arm, his fingers like a pincer digging into my flesh even as I bent to pick up my suitcase with the other hand. As he started pulling me towards the train, I called "Shalom" to my friends. The pressure on my arm increased and did not stop until we were well away from the boys.

Then he dropped his hand and spoke in a voice icy with anger and each word a separate accusation, "You will compromise my plan. You will destroy both of us!"

"What did I say?" My cry was from the heart, but it sounded like whining. I would never have recognized my own voice. Next, I tried an explanation, "Those boys are with B'richa themselves."

"Hush! You talk too much!" With his free hand across his stomach and a pained grimace on his face, he limped ahead of me through the crowds. I had to concentrate hard on following him or I would have lost him altogether in the noisy swarm of people, as thick as a forest in its darkest part.

Suddenly, I saw a small, swarthy man in rags grab him by his good arm. He tried to shake himself loose, but he was unable to free himself. As I got nearer, I heard the smaller man shouting emotionally in a language I did not understand.

My father answered him in German. "What are you talking about? You are mistaken, I tell you. Now leave me alone." The man held onto my father's arm with two hands.

My father spied me with a look of relief. "Hella! Hella! Come here. Tell this man who we are. We are German Jews, you hear? Let me go!"

The man's mouth fell open as he regarded me with eyes almost black at their center.

Letting go of my father's arm, the gypsy turned to his companion, a woman bending towards him with every word of his reflected in the emotions on her face. Now his eyes were full of confusion. I knew that look. I had seen it on the faces of the people in the camp when memory and reality blended, the past intermixing with the present, the eyes clouding over with their own strange reality.

The moment the gypsy's hands fell, my father pushed me forward into the crowd. Without looking back, he led me away, panting, perspiration beading his face.

He didn't stop until we were in the midst of the throng before the train. As he mopped his face with a handkerchief, the train made a sudden short noise and lurched forward. A shout went up from the crowd.

Faces appeared in the windows of the train, the steps to it were mobbed, and it seemed impossible for anyone else to get on. *We'll have to wait for another,* I thought. But my father picked up the satchel he had momentarily rested on the ground and continued pushing his way forward.

"Do we have tickets?" I asked him.

"Of course we have tickets. And we're getting on this train. You go first so I don't keep banging my arm."

It was impossible for him to keep his arm out of the way, and it seemed to pain him whenever it was touched. Still, we pressed forward, sometimes shoving our way around people who would not move for us, sometimes leaning against them until they gave way for us. Finally, we were at the train's steps, but I couldn't imagine how two more human beings could possibly get aboard.

He seemed to read my mind. "We must get on," he said.

The train whistle blew. In desperation, I pressed against the people on the steps, stepping on feet, elbowing their bodies, falling on them, their curses in my ears and their fists rammed against my side as I managed to climb on the steps with my father right in back of me, shoving me on.

Half-expecting to be beaten and pushed off, I somehow managed to make my way to the top of the steps. Glancing back at the surge of humanity leaning in the direction of the train like stalks of wheat in the wind, I could make out the gypsy who had stopped my father, trying to get through the crowds, pointing to the steps where we stood, as the woman with him trailed behind him, her eyes lifted towards us. My father noticed him, too, and I felt him push me farther inside the train where the darkness and the narrow space brought me back to the heavy wooden chest in the Burgers' apartment. Herman had insisted that I practice hiding in it in case the Gestapo came around. I crouched silently at the bottom with pains shooting through my cramped legs. There, like here, I felt the sides closing in on me, the space above and the space below moving together. And when I opened my mouth to scream, no sound came out.

## CHAPTER FIVE

# Interrupted Journey

Noise roared in my ears as the floor hit the ceiling. I felt hot. I felt cold. And when I opened my eyes, I was in a compartment on a bench, my father was next to me, and a man with dark hair was struggling to open the window. With a squeak, the window opened about a fifth of the way, and the rush of air felt good on my face.

"Keep your head between your legs," my father advised me.

I kept my head down until the roaring in my ears ceased altogether.

"I'm all right," I said, sitting up.

The man struggled with the window, but it would go up no farther. He cursed in Italian, then turned to me. In a softer voice, he asked me something I couldn't understand. I guessed it was about how I was feeling, so I responded with a weak smile, and he nodded with satisfaction, returning to his seat next to my father.

Across from us sat a family of three, a man, a wife and a daughter in her early twenties, I guessed. All of them had round faces and beady eyes, as though they were mass produced, although the father and daughter's eyes were brown and the mother's blue. I wondered if the man and the woman grew to look alike or if they married each other because each thought the other's appearance so beautiful.

Now the woman leaned towards me. "You feel better?" she asked.

"Yes," I replied, but my father gave her such an angry glance that her face reddened, and she straightened up in

51

her seat and turned to gaze at her daughter, showing him that she had her own family and did not have to bother with us.

With a screech, the train jerked forward, then slowly started moving out of the station. Outside, people were shouting and thrusting themselves forward.

Other young people from the displaced persons camp had described how they traveled by hoisting themselves through open windows, then scampering around to avoid the ticket takers. With the word, "Amcho" they identified themselves as Jews, so that any of their people inside would help them.

Sure enough, Jack was holding on to the window, straining to fit through it. Jumping up, I strained to open it more, but I was unsuccessful. "I can't," I muttered in frustration before Jack jumped down.

"What are you doing?" my father demanded.

I stepped away from the window so he could see it was empty. Although I couldn't imagine him disapproving of my helping Jack, I thought it better not to say anything in front of the others.

"The window won't open any further," I replied.

"It's too cool in here," complained the Austrian girl as I sat.

When I glanced out the window again, Jack had disappeared from view in the crowd still surging against the rolling train. Some of them outside banged their fists against the train as it moved past them, others threw rocks. Luckily, none hit us or the window of our compartment. Now we were gathering speed, and in a few minutes, the town of Landsberg was behind us. Before long, we were in the countryside, in fields untouched by the war, passing cows and goats who grazed peacefully, without a glance at the roaring train.

My father was at the window. "Look, Hella," he said, as the train ran along a stream shaded with trees, their leaves of brilliant reds and yellows. "Such beauty," he murmured, as my heart swelled with contentment from our sharing the moment. "A person can breathe here."

But at Munich, the people who could not get on the train blocked the tracks, and it was more than an hour before we could go again. Only away from the cities, it seemed, the train ran without trouble.

For lunch, the Austrian family got busy with a knit bag from which they took out wurst and bread which they ate with lip-smacking noises for a while before my father removed neatly-wrapped cheese and bread from his satchel. In a moment, the compartment became pungent with the aroma of food. The Italian watched us with wide eyes, swallowed once and looked away.

My eyes met my father's. He could read my mind. "Don't be a fool," he muttered. "Give away cheese today, and you'll eat dirt tomorrow."

I supposed he was right, but I could not face the Italian. Instead, I turned to look out the window as I ate. We were passing through a forest of pine trees now. Beyond the trees, rising like a huge wave, were snow-capped mountains.

My father finished eating, dusted the crumbs from his hands, then carefully wiped his fingers on his handkerchief and sat back. I had finished, too.

For the first time, I relaxed to the steady sound and movement of the train. I thought of how my life had changed since yesterday in Landsberg! *Who would have known? Who could have guessed?* Yet, in a way it was not so strange. In my daydreams, meeting my father always led me to some strange and wonderful adventure, ending in the Holy Land, of course. *And here I was already on a train, the first important step in a long journey.*

I glanced at my father, sitting next to me, straight as before and obviously deep in thought.

"Papa," I began hesitantly. "Tell me about when you were a little boy."

He thought for a moment. "I always wanted to be a doctor," he began.

"Yes?" I sat forward. Telling me about his life would be a gift as real as sharing his food with me or buying me a precious train ticket.

He glanced at the Austrians, now finished with their lunches, the father and daughter beginning to nap, the mother reading a tattered Bible. "Some other time," he said with an impatient wave of his hand.

Disappointed, I turned from him. *Always some other time. Perhaps he didn't love me, at least not the way he loved Ruth. She had remembered when they arrested him, and she had even remembered our lives before then, while I hardly recalled him at all. But, still, I loved my father,* I thought, the tears welling up in my eyes.

In my most despairing moments, the hope of finding him gave me courage and purpose. In the D.P. camp where I was busy with classes, with our "kibbutz" and with volunteering in the hospital, every night before sleep I thought of my father, creating lovely visions of our lives together that eased me into calm dreams.

"We will be together again," my mother had reassured us time and time again. "You'll see."

Even when our Jewish neighbors were getting visas to America or leaving for France or Holland, Mama refused to abandon our father, saying, "How will he find us in another country? It's better if we wait for him here, and then we'll leave together."

Every day, when I was still little, our neighbors' sons and fathers were released from jails and detention camps. One day, our papa would be released, too, we believed, and we would lose no time in leaving Germany for good.

Closing my eyes, I let myself sway to the rhythm of the train, as I drifted into sleep. When the train braked sharply to a stop, I awakened. My father was standing by the window, trying to see what was ahead of us.

"Why did we stop?" I asked him.

"Another train is being routed to our track." He straightened up. "You stay here and watch my bag," he told me. "Don't open it, understand?" His tone was unexpectedly sharp.

All I had ever seen in the bag was food, and I felt insulted that he did not trust me with it. Still, my answer was respectful, "Yes, Papa."

When he left, I glanced out the window, surprised to see the sun an orange ball now, dipping low in the sky. It reminded me of a promise I had made to my friend.

*I miss you so, Margot,* I thought. I closed my eyes to concentrate better, going over the day's adventures, just as I would have if she were there. When I finished, I tried to hear her voice. What would she say?

*You've gone far, Hella, dear. Now you must try to understand your father. Be patient, be strong, be well. Remember me.*

For a moment, her voice and my mother's had merged into one gentle, protecting spirit.

Opening my eyes again just as my father returned to the compartment, I realized the train was starting up with hisses and squeaks.

"Give me your identification paper," he told me as he sat again. "I don't want to have to awaken you if we pass the border while you're sleeping."

That was thoughtful of him. "Thank you," I murmured as I handed the document to him. At the camp in Landsberg, we had been given a paper that served as our passport. I had kept it in my pocket for the journey.

That night I dreamt about meeting Margot along the way, and when I awoke, it was almost dawn. The train was stopped in the midst of a wide field. Everyone else was sleeping, so I rose very quietly, planning to relieve myself in some secluded spot away from the train, for the bathroom on the train was filthy, then return as quickly as possible.

Some people were already sitting on the steps of the train, some were on the ground. One young man standing on the grass and smoking helped me off by giving me his hand as I stepped down. "Be careful," he warned me in Yiddish, and I thanked him in the same language.

The morning air was fresh, and beads of dew clung to every blade of grass. When I returned, I looked among the people sitting and standing about, hoping to spot Jack and Norbert, but they were not there. They probably had not made the train, I guessed, but the young man who had helped me down the steps was still there. This time he held out a canteen for me.

"Would you care for some water?" he asked.

My throat was parched, and I hadn't washed at all, so the water was doubly welcome. I drank some and asked if I could use a handful for washing.

"Certainly," he replied graciously. "Where are you going?" he asked when I returned the canteen.

For a moment, the question stumped me, for I was not supposed to reveal our destination. "Uh—Austria," I stammered.

He smiled. "We're in Austria already. We passed Innsbruck in the middle of the night."

"South Austria, then."

"Where are you from?" His brown eyes were friendly, and he had a way of speaking I found pleasant. Besides, I was in no hurry to return to the ill-smelling train.

"I was living in the camp in Landsberg, but I was born in Berlin."

His face lit up when I said that. "Me, too. Grosse Hamburger Strasse."

"Yes!" I exclaimed. I was sure that was near where I lived, in the Wilmersdorf section. "That sounds so familiar." My voice rose with excitement.

Meeting someone from what was my home and neighborhood was finding a witness to my life and all that once was mine—my mailman, my grocer, my teacher. If our memories were similar, then they were valid. They were more than dreams.

"We had a dry goods store. Our apartment was over it. Do you recall Kruger's Dry Goods?" he asked.

There were stores nearby, of course. But except for a chicken market alive with fowl and a store that sold candy, I couldn't remember them. I shook my head.

"My name is Karl Kruger," the young man continued. "What's yours?"

"Hella Weiss. My mother's name was Dora..."

"Ruth must have been your sister. She played the harp, right?"

Now I clapped my hands together. "That's right."

Near us, the train made a grinding sound, then lurched forward.

Without pausing in his narrative, Karl jumped on the steps, and again put out a hand to help me. "Your mother and mine were friends. They used to go to concerts together. I'll never forget a fur boa your mother wore, with the head of a fox. Remember?"

"I remember. It used to scare me."

"And I was appalled by it," he added, as we both laughed at the memory.

The train was starting up again. We had to move farther into it as others were coming aboard from the fields. Now Karl's face became serious. "Are any of them alive?"

I almost said my father, but I stopped myself in time, and told him instead what I knew about my mother and Ruth. "I hid out with the Burgers. Do you remember Maria Burger, the pharmacist?"

Before he had a chance to answer, my father appeared.

"Hella!" he shouted in a voice that seemed to make my blood run cold.

He glanced at Karl, but neither showed any sign of recognition. *Karl must have been a child when he last saw my father,* I thought. *After so many wretched years, my father must have changed terribly.*

I had to make some introduction. "This is my uncle from Munich," I said. "And this is Karl Kruger whose family owned a dry goods store on Grosse Hamburger Strasse. He knew..." I almost said "Mama." *Should I say it?* "...my family." I ended with my voice faltering.

With a slight bow to Karl and no change in his harsh expression, my father took my arm, his fingers digging into my flesh. "Excuse me," he said to Karl. "One cannot be too careful about to whom a young girl speaks on a train." Then, addressing me, "Come, I was distraught looking for you," he shouted above the grinding noise of the train's wheels against the tracks. Without another word, he began pulling me, not too gently, back to our compartment.

"I'll see you later, Hella," Karl called after me, but now I was afraid even to wave good-bye to him, for hadn't I done it again? Hadn't I directed attention to my father and myself exactly as he had told me repeatedly not to?

"Wait! Wait!" Karl shouted in back of us. My father stopped and we turned together. Karl was making his way towards us, his eyes on my father's tight grip on my arm. "Is everything all right?" he asked me.

"Yes. My fath...," I stopped myself in time, luckily, for my father was already glaring at me. "My uncle is very strict. As he said, he doesn't like me to speak to strangers."

Karl seemed very poised and kind as he answered. "I'm not a stranger, Hella. I knew your whole family," he reminded me gently. "Please, remember, if I can help you..."

"Thank you, Karl."

Taking his cue from Karl's behavior, my father dropped his hand from my arm and attempted a reassuring smile, but the smile immediately got twisted into something more like a grimace. As much as I would have liked to continue speaking to Karl, I couldn't go against my father's wishes.

I turned to our compartment, and Karl turned in the opposite direction. But before we entered the close and oppressive little room, my father grabbed me by the shoulders. Without a word, he shook me again and again, my body flopping like a rag doll's.

Once, on the farm, when the manager found a cow wandering in the neighboring pasture because of my daydreaming, he shook me like that. He sent me to sleep without supper, but I had hidden some eggs in the barn under the hay, and I ate those, seasoning the warm liquid with the salt of my tears. "Boruch atoh adonoy," I prayed over the eggs in rebellion, forgetting most of the prayer when it would have been far safer not to remember any of it.

When my father finished shaking me, I stumbled on rubbery legs to my seat. The Austrian girl glanced at me first with surprise, then with a smug look of satisfaction. *I'm not going to cry,* I told myself. *I'm thirteen and girls my age are carrying guns in Palestine to protect their land, but he has no right to shake me like that.*

I closed my eyes. How I wished I were in Palestine already! I began daydreaming about my father's leaving me on the kibbutz in Palestine while he returned on a mission to Europe. I had to carry on without him, making important decisions for many people. For comfort, I added Margot to the kibbutz...when Karl appeared at the door of our compartment.

"There you are, Hella!" he exclaimed.

I sat up, glancing at my father whose feelings I guessed by his sharp intake of breath and flaring nostrils. Yet I could tell that Karl was trustworthy. A former neighbor, a friend of the family's, and a Jew, how could he jeopardize our journey? And my father hadn't trusted Margot, Jack or Norbert. Did he think they were all British informers?

"Hello," I greeted Karl.

"Hello, again," my father said, deliberately keeping his voice pleasant. He was attempting to be charming as he had before, first with Margot, when he was explaining why she could not come with us, then, for a moment, with Jack and Norbert before he pulled me away from them. I realized it was a mask he donned, and his performance was usually followed by a burst of anger, like some temperamental actor's tantrum.

Karl indicated the empty spot next to me, left by the Italian's departure. "May I come in for a minute?"

Before my father could answer, Karl was in our compartment.

Of course, I would have loved to reminisce with Karl about our old neighborhood, and, especially, my mother. We hadn't even discussed his family yet. Perhaps I would remember some of them. But I knew how unwelcome his presence was to my father.

*Karl was a nice young man I met on the train. Soon we both would get off, and I probably would never see him again. My father and I would be together forever,* I thought.

"I'm sorry, Karl." Glancing at my father, for his approval, I told Karl, "I'm really not feeling well. I'd better rest."

"I understand," he replied with disappointment in his voice. "I'm sorry if I disturbed you." He turned, but then halted at the doorway and turned back to us. There was a mischievous gleam in his eye. "Would a piece of chocolate make you feel better?"

*Would it!* "Oh, yes!" No one ever made as quick a recovery.

Reaching into the bag he carried, he took out half a bar of chocolate, rewrapped carefully. He broke off a rectangular piece, and handed it to me. The rest of the bar he offered to my father, who shook his head.

My third piece of chocolate! The other two had been given to me by American soldiers, one right after liberation by the young driver of a jeep who warned us to eat it slowly so it would not sicken our fragile stomachs, and the second by Sergeant de Fillippi, for my pretty green eyes, he said.

But the moment Karl was out the door, my father shook his finger at me. "I don't want you speaking to him again."

Savoring the sweet taste in my mouth, I asked, "Why not?"

My question infuriated him. "You don't know anything. I'm telling you not to talk to him again. Or see him. That's all. No explanations. Do you understand?"

No, I didn't understand. And I wanted to, because the idea that I had to obey a man who was being unreasonable just because he told me to disturbed me. "Did you know Karl's family back home? Is that why?"

Springing to his feet a moment before the train suddenly braked to a halt threw him off-balance. He regained his balance and hovered over me. For a moment, I thought he might slap me. *No,* flashed through my mind, *not in front of the Austrian girl!* But instead, he punished me with his words.

"I should have left you in Landsberg! You are a great burden to me, Hella, not a help at all." Stomping past me, he peered out the window. We were at a station in the midst of a rural area. His arm shot up, and he pulled his satchel from its place overhead. "Take your valise and follow me. We're going! Hurry!"

*Going?* I hesitated. We were in a small hamlet, nowhere near our destination, as far as I could tell.

"Come along. Now," he demanded.

Reluctantly, I followed him.

My father turned in the direction opposite the one where I had met Karl. The corridor was crowded now with travelers wanting to get off for some fresh air or for the water fountain, and my father lifted his satchel high above his head while I followed him, squeezing myself and my valise through the throng. But I could hardly keep up with him.

As I rushed after him, I suddenly realized that I didn't have to get off with him. *Karl could tell me what to do to return to Landsberg. Perhaps I could even find Jack and Norbert on board. Eventually, I would get to Palestine with my friends, with Margot and Olga and Esther. Or I could find out where Karl was going and travel with him....*

"Hurry, hurry," my father admonished me from up ahead. Between us were an odd assortment of men and women from Germany, Austria, Italy and God only knew where else. In a moment, they would be cursing me for pushing them out of my way.

"Hurry!"

"I'm coming," I answered in the same impatient tone.

*He is difficult and demanding,* I thought. *He treats me like a child even though I have taken good care of myself for years. But he is my father. And he is leading me to Palestine so much sooner than I had imagined. I will never forgive myself if I lost him now after the miracle of finding him.*

*I am too independent from being on my own. That's clear. And he must still imagine me as the toddler he had left at home. If only time could be reversed and those lost years relived.*

On the steps where some peasants were pushing their way on, getting off was even more difficult. I leaned against one woman until she gave way, punching a boy about my size who punched me first in the ribs. I was almost off when I was pushed back, intimidated by a husky farmer. Already on the ground, my father grabbed my arm and pulled me off the steps from the side. I fell, bruising my knee and elbow.

Immediately his finger was pointing angrily at me. "You are to keep your mouth shut. Understand? I will do all the talking for both of us."

My heart sank. Forgetting the stinging pain of my bruises, the thought most prominent in my mind was, *Why did I follow him?* He was my father, true, and my happiest moment was finding him. But I disliked him. *Yes.* That was a terrible truth, but it was the truth. I disliked my own father. And I could survive without him, just as I did during the war when the danger was as close as shells shrieking in my ears or German soldiers questioning me about my patriotism.

His eyes followed mine to the train. He knew what I was thinking. "I have your passport," he reminded me. He grabbed my valise. "Come on," he barked at me. Confident that my only choice was following him, he marched off.

When I looked back at the train, I saw Jack at one of the windows near me. He gestured his surprise, but I couldn't communicate with him except to show that I too was surprised not to be on the train, and I didn't know what my father had in mind.

My father was now a good dozen steps away from me. There was still time to run and catch up with him and return to the train. But I had to have my passport, at least that.

Swerving around the crowds, I ran after him crying, "Please, Papa. Please give me my things."

As he kept walking, I kept imploring him. "I can go with Jack. He's on the train. Or I can go back to Landsberg. I won't say a word about your mission. You'll be rid of me...till Palestine. Please!"

He did not even glance my way, but continued walking to the end of the station. The train's wheels started turning, throwing off sparks. With the noise of the train, he probably couldn't even hear me as I shouted, "Please. I need my passport."

Finally he stopped and turned to me just as the train started to roll. If he gave me the passport now, I could still make it.

Putting the bags he was carrying on the ground, he bent over his satchel to unbuckle it.

Meanwhile, I continued my promises, "I'll keep every secret you told me. I swear. I'll never speak about this whole incident." *And we'll meet in Palestine some day and be close then,* I thought. But there was no time to speak anymore, for he was taking out a folded paper from his satchel.

I stood with one hand on my valise and the other held out for the paper. Instead of giving it to me, he opened it. It was not my passport, after all. It was only a map.

When he glanced back at me, his cold eyes mocked my distress.

Jack and Norbert's car, with the two boys leaning out the window, was far ahead now. The last car of the train was about to pass, and it was too far for me to catch, even if I had my passport. Covered with a film of sweat, I shivered. When I looked at my father, he was studying me.

"Do you want to run away?" he asked, his blue eyes as cold as marble. "My own daughter? Shame on you."

Both of us watched the train leaving the little station. "Too late," he said, laughing.

And, I realized with a shudder, that was the very first time I had heard him laugh.

## CHAPTER SIX

# Let The Stranger Live!

With a long, thin finger, he traced a route on the map. Although I knew he was displeased with me, I was too curious to keep still. "Where are we?" I asked.

Folding the map carefully, he replied, "If you didn't blabber to every boy you met, we would still be on the train. I'm not telling you anything anymore." He placed the map back in the satchel, buckled the case closed, and started walking. With a heavy heart, I followed him.

I had an answer for him, but speaking to him now would only anger him further, so I kept my defense to myself: *Jack and Norbert could be trusted. Weren't they our comrades in escaping to Palestine? And I never said a word to Karl about our true destination or that I was with my father. I was trustworthy. I didn't blabber*, I thought, kicking a stone that lay on the dirt road.

Soon we were in a wide meadow where cows grazed. Dotting the scene were storage barns, their weathered wood as gray as the mountains that loomed about us.

I overtook my father, then led the way, daydreaming about assisting him at a hospital in Palestine. I could only work mornings, for I had classes of my own in medical studies. Naturally, I would have had to skip many grades, and so I was addressing the panel of teachers who would determine the grade in which I was to start, when something made me stop and turn. My father was nowhere in sight!

I looked down the road and at the fields, but there was no sign of him there. With a feeling of panic rising from my gut and filling my mouth with a bitter taste, I started back the way I came.

A good quarter mile back from where I had walked, beyond a turn in the road, I spotted him under a tree. The fear turned to anger.

*Is this his idea of a joke—to let me walk on needlessly when we still had so many miles to go? Is he still punishing me for speaking to Karl? What kind of father is he? Has he lost all the compassion my mother had lovingly praised him for?*

*Not all of the reunions I saw were happy,* I recalled as I trudged towards him, my legs growing as heavy as logs, my feet pinched in my shoes. I remembered the curses of the strange girl who had been in our kibbutz at Landsberg for only a day. "The old witch!" she called her mother, shocking us, for most of us were orphans, our dear mothers wrenched away or parted from us for our own safety in what were the worst moments of our lives.

"You go to Palestine, not me. I'm no Jew!" the girl announced to us in Yiddish.

She had lived during the war with a Christian family who had treated her as one of their own. At the end of the war, a woman she hardly knew, her true mother, took her away from the comforts of her home and newer family to wander as a refugee, searching for a younger brother she didn't remember. *No, not all reunions are happy.*

As I neared my father, I decided what I would tell him, right to his face. "Hurting me can't possibly help you," I would say, speaking like a grown-up.

But when I reached him, my anger faded like the mist of morning.

Bending over his arm, he was grimacing with pain. "It's throbbing terribly," he said.

"Do you want me to change the dressing?"

"Yes."

*How could I tell him my thoughts when he was suffering already? No, I'll wait,* I thought.

Opening his satchel, he took out a towel I recognized from the infirmary and placed soap, a bandage, tape, a small scissors and the salve on it. First, he made me wash my hands with the water from his canteen, then he directed me in removing the old dressing, which must have been excruciating to him, although he bore the pain with only a well-controlled gasp. His injury was raw, blistering and still hot to the touch, but I had seen much worse cases of infection, and the salve and new bandage seemed to soothe his pain.

He was in a better mood when he started walking again. "You have good hands. You could be a nurse."

My heart dropped down to my dusty shoes. *Nurse?* I remembered Mama's encouragement, "You have the intelligence to be a doctor, and I know you'll have the talent, too, as great as your sister's in music. Just like Papa."

Evidently, Papa wouldn't agree.

"I don't want to be a nurse," I said. "I want to be a doctor like you."

"A doctor?" he scoffed. "Women are not capable of being good doctors. They have moods. They get hysterical. And who will care for your own children?"

"Didn't you ever work with a woman doctor?"

"They were freaks, not real women with husbands and children. A woman's place is in the home."

We were walking uphill, my legs aching with the strain, my breaths getting shorter, as his were, as we climbed.

He gasped out the rest of his argument. "A woman has to raise her sons and teach her daughters how to care for the house. Otherwise her children will run wild. Any other way is unnatural."

"What about Palestine?" I reminded him. "Where the women work alongside the men?"

He had no answer for that, except an annoyed wave of his hand. "That's different."

My heart thumped heavily with the thought of challenging him, repeating what Mama had said, but he was huffing and puffing so painfully, I decided it was better not to argue with him anymore. We continued on in silence, stopping frequently to rub our legs and to rest.

When the sun was almost directly overhead, we came to a town with narrow cobbled streets and high-peaked houses; designs, once-colorful, now faded and chipped, were painted on their fronts. The aroma of an inn drew my father to its door, but before we entered, he grabbed me by the arm and barked in my ear. "Remember, silence!"

Inside, men who were obviously farmers and a variety of travelers were sitting, eating, talking noisily and drinking beer at small wooden tables. As we sat, I recalled that Maria Burger always said how dirty the Austrians were, and I wondered what the darkness hid.

But that didn't stop me from downing the thin soup my father ordered for me, explaining, "It is good for you." I hungered for some of the wurst and cabbage on his plate, but I wouldn't dare ask him for any. As I watched him eat, though, he passed some of his bread to me.

70

When he had finished, he rose with a beer stein in hand and approached a table of farmers. Above the din, I heard the names of towns and distances. "Matrei am Brenner," "Steinach," "Gries." Returning to the table, he gestured that we were leaving.

Outside, one of the farmers who had been at the table led us to his horse and cart. The farmer was in his thirties, I guessed, tall and lanky as a scarecrow, with curly brown hair, and a polite manner of speaking to me that I liked.

My father patted the horse's nose, and spoke to her with joking affection. I had never seen him so gentle before, and I felt glad to recognize feelings I had, also, for the animals had been my only friends on the farm. With them, I relaxed, the chickens and pigs when I fed them, the cows when I led them to pasture, the horses that nuzzled me as I groomed them.

My father addressed the farmer. "This mare must have taken you many kilometers," he said.

"So she has," the farmer agreed.

Since there was not room for the three of us up front, I climbed into the wagon part, which still smelled from the earth and the potatoes it had carried to market.

Up front, the farmer was talking about horses. *He was a real talker,* I thought. But my father surprised me by encouraging him and answering him. He was more patient with the farmer than anyone else I had seen him with.

Rubbing my aching legs, the steady shaking of the wagon suddenly jogged my memory. I was very little, for my father was still at home. It must have been a Sunday or a holiday when my family and Herman and Maria packed a box of food and crowded into Papa's car for a drive to a park. My father and Herman were standing and talking near a pond, and I was crouched a few feet away, playing with some

71

leaves and twigs. Suddenly, a bee stung my arm. The pain was so sharp and unexpected that I cried partly from the shock of the attack. My father reassured me and patted cool mud on my arm. When we returned home, Papa washed off the mud and kissed the welt the bee's sting had left.

"Now you are all cured," he told me, and I finally did feel all better.

Despite the bee sting, it was a beautiful memory. *I'll have to ask him later if he recalls that,* I thought.

The steady clomp of the horse and the motion of the wagon soon put me to sleep. When I awoke, we were on a steep incline on the side of the mountain which loomed above us like some fearful monster. When I looked down, the view so far below took my breath away! For one terrible moment, I pictured the horse stumbling on a rock and the cart I was in breaking loose and tumbling, tumbling down.

I couldn't bear to look down and tried to stop myself from thinking about what could happen, for the road was becoming even narrower, and one misstep could hurtle us over the edge. Shivering with cold, I looked longingly at my suitcase which had slid to the far end of the wagon. Although I had some warmer clothes packed away, I was afraid to move around in the open wagon, so I only huddled closer to the front, where the men were still talking.

"Hitler never should have invaded Russia," my father was saying, "and I underestimated the Americans."

I had heard that discussion endlessly at Landsberg, and I was about to lose myself, continuing the pleasant daydream of my life in Palestine, when the word "Nuremberg" caught my attention. Trials of high German war criminals were set to begin soon in that city, the first time in history that the conquerors of a nation were allowing the defeated, who had started the long nightmare, the benefit of a fair, democratic trial. Before I had left camp, there had been talk of little else. Many of the refugees felt that even shooting mass murderers when they were flushed out of hiding was too kind a punishment. But some welcomed the trials. Time and time again, friends marked for death begged the others to tell the world what had happened to them. I had heard of many who had hung onto a life more bitter than poison only to bear witness for the sake of justice. What better way than at a public trial of the war criminals?

"Justice. Ha! When the victors choose the prosecutors and defense?" my father was saying.

We had discussed this very point in our kibbutz, and I thought I could debate it logically. "Don't you think there should be trials?" I shouted, so they could hear me up front.

"Quiet, child!" my father ordered me. He had turned around to address me, and I recognized that white anger on his face, his icicle eyes and the lined brow above them. When he turned back to the farmer, I leaned uncomfortably against the wooden slats of the wagon's side, my face red and hot from his latest insult.

I could say nothing, obviously, for I still was a child to him, incapable of even making a comment in his adult world. Yet working in the hospital, taking part in my kibbutz, I was taken seriously, even by grownups. I did not enter discussions lightly, only when I thought my ideas were as substantial as bread and milk, and then people listened. Not my father. He considered me a fool, although he couldn't know how his contempt wounded me.

I crossed my arms and hugged myself for warmth. Still, we climbed. The scene itself was awesome, I decided, becoming brave enough to look down at the road far below, curling like a river.

My father was dozing, now, and the farmer singing quietly, then lapsing into long silences as we alternately ascended, then leveled off.

As we entered a town, around dinnertime, the farmer pulled his horse to a halt. My father opened his eyes, and, realizing we had stopped, sat up with a jolt. "Where are we?"

"Steinach," replied the farmer. "This is as far as I go. I have to get back to my farm tonight."

"I want to get to the Pass," my father answered, angrily. "I thought that was clear."

The farmer didn't answer and we didn't move.

"I'll pay you extra to keep going."

The farmer's tone was just as adamant as my father's. "Just give me what you promised. I have to return to my farm."

My father opened his satchel, to get the money, I assumed, but he took out something else, something that made the farmer gasp.

"What's this?" the man asked in dismay.

"Keep going. I don't want trouble, but I have to get to the border. You keep going." Lifting the object in his hand higher, I saw that he held a gun.

Involuntarily, I let out a groan.

"Keep out of this, Hella," he warned me without a glance in my direction. The farmer hadn't even strapped his horse to get it moving again, and my father muttered to him, "Now. I'm not waiting." Then as an afterthought, he added, "And don't try to take the gun away from me. I'll kill you first." His voice was as cold and as clear as the streams along the side of the road, and I didn't doubt him for a minute.

The farmer who had sung so freely started up his horse with a slap of his reins and a choked command. The horse started to walk. In a moment, we were passing through the quiet town of Steinach at a trot.

I kept my eyes on the both of them, for if for some reason my father dropped his gun, the farmer might grab it and shoot us both. The least he would do would be to turn us over to the authorities, and God only knew what they would do to us, for my father's cause, although great, was illegal.

I sat so stiffly that my arms, legs and back began to ache, and every movement of the wagon stabbed me with pain. I was afraid to watch my father with the gun in his hand and afraid not to. Luckily, no one else was on the road. Yet, so many things could still go wrong. I started to pray, *Please, God, spare the farmer's life. And see us safely to the end of this nightmare.*

## CHAPTER SEVEN

# Who Is He?

Was my father capable of killing the man? I didn't know. The father I remembered faintly, like the shadows of a dream in mid-afternoon, brought us little hard candies sweet to the taste. He read us fairy tales at night, then tucked us under our blankets with a soft, "Sweet dreams."

In all the years we were apart, I had idealized him as the perfect father, believing, as Mama did, that he would return to save us. He would be our shelter, and everything bad would turn all right in the soothing comfort of his care.

Later, when things became hopeless, I resented him. I agreed with Ruth when she cried, "Why did he have to get himself arrested? Why did they keep him when they let other men go? He abandoned us."

But that was not what I held against him now. He was gruffer, less affectionate, less interested in me, more impatient and ill-tempered than I ever imagined. And unpredictable. Would he pull the trigger on the farmer? How could I answer? I didn't even know that he carried a gun.

After a while, when I could make out some lights and the outlines of homes against the darkening sky, I sighed out loud with relief.

"What town is that?" I asked.

"Gries," the farmer answered. "The Brenner Pass is a short hike ahead."

"Take me to lodgings," my father ordered him.

"Yes. I don't want trouble." The farmer's voice was different now, restrained, as though he were afraid of speaking too glibly. "I want to get back to my farm."

My father studied him, as my breath seemed to congeal in a knot in my chest.

"I have to feed the animals," the farmer said.

"When I find a place for the night, you can go, my friend," my father answered him.

Now there were people on the street. Worrying that the farmer might cry out for help, I was relieved when he silently pulled his horse to a stop in front of an old house with an unreadable wooden sign hanging above its door.

"Hella, see if there are lodgings for the night," my father told me, without taking his eyes off the farmer.

My back and legs sore from the long ride, I jumped down from the wagon and knocked on the door of the inn. When no one answered, I banged even harder. *Please, someone come,* I prayed, *so my father will let the farmer go.*

A middle-aged man, shaped wide in the middle like a child's top, opened the door.

"Do you have a room for my father and me for the night?"

He grunted something that sounded like, "Yes," and I returned to the cart with my message.

"I'll pay you," my father murmured to the farmer as he started to open his satchel. I was relieved to see him slip the gun into the pocket of his coat before climbing down. I scurried to the back for my suitcase. No sooner did my father put his foot on the ground than the farmer strapped his horse and took off, disappearing at a gallop into the darkness.

Something on the street caught my attention. I bent down to pick it up thinking, *it can't be!* Yet, it was. The red and yellow scarf that Margot always wore, or at least one exactly like it, I thought, as I held it closer to study it. Margot's was even ripped and sewn in the same place. *What is it doing here?*

My father was watching me from the doorway of the inn. "What have you got?"

"Just a scarf," I replied, picturing how he would scoff if I told him I thought it was Margot's.

Glancing at it disdainfully, he warned me, "Wash it before you put it near any of my things."

As we followed the innkeeper up to our room, I tried to come up with an explanation for the scarf. *Since Margot is still in Landsberg, it can't possibly be hers, yet it is exactly like hers, even the repair. Mass produced, perhaps all of the scarves have a weakness at the same seam. Or maybe it got stuck in my suitcase and I didn't notice it until it fell out. No. That's ridiculous.* But however it came to me, whoever had owned it, I was glad I found it. It would comfort me with thoughts of my friend.

*My friend!* As I held the scarf against my cheek, I realized that it was already dark, and I had failed to think of her at sunset. *I'm sorry, Margot,* I thought.

The room the innkeeper brought us to was large, but sparsely furnished with one narrow bed and mattress, a cot, and a frequently repaired, once-elegant chair. Near the door was a chipped and stained sink. A window with a thin, ripped curtain on the far side of the room looked down onto the street. Nearby was a tavern with some horses and their wagons tied in front.

After we washed our hands and faces, my father, seated on the chair, took supper out from the satchel—bread, now hardening, which he shared with me, and a can of sardines. Swallowing my saliva, I sat next to him on the floor watching him eat the pungent sardines. Before he was finished, I complained that I was still hungry, and he handed me the can with one small fish remaining.

Gathering my courage, I asked him, "Is that all?"

"That's all for now," he replied gruffly. "Tomorrow we'll be in Italy. There will be fruits and olives and many good things to eat. You'll see."

Before I could say anything else, he stood. "I'm going out," he announced. "Now don't you go speaking to anyone," he warned me, shaking a finger in my face. "And don't go near my satchel. Don't touch it. Understand?"

What else could I say? "Yes, Papa."

As he put on his raincoat, he gave me another warning. "Stay in the room. Don't go walking around."

I nodded.

"Go to sleep," he ordered me from the doorway.

But I had slept in the cart, and I wasn't tired. Opening my suitcase, I took out the music box Margot had given me. To the strains of "The Blue Danube," I gazed out the window at the street below, illuminated with a light above the door of the inn and a lamp in front of the tavern.

*How straight my father's posture is, like a person's never beaten or starved. So unusual.* Then, I thought with a sigh, *my father is unusual.* Mama always said that he forged paths others couldn't even see, but I never realized how difficult it would be for me to follow him.

Despite his orders to stay inside the room, I had to leave it to use the toilet in the hall. Afterwards, thinking about the miracle of finding Margot's scarf, which I kept tied around my neck now, I decided to ask the innkeeper if he had seen anyone resembling Margot. I didn't know which was his room.

"Innkeeper!" I called out loud in the hallway. "Innkeeper!"

The door from another room opened, but instead of the Austrian innkeeper, a flat-faced, bare-chested man in his twenties stepped into the hallway. He seemed surprised, then happy to see me. Speaking in a dialect I did not understand, Croatian, perhaps, he stepped towards me, a dirty hand beckoning me to come with him. Frightened, I returned to my room and quickly locked the door.

Again, I went to the window. *No sign of my father outside, but,* I thought, *there's no doubt about his returning,* · *for didn't he leave his precious satchel?*

That reminded me of the identification paper I had used as a passport. I had to get it, no matter what he said, for without it, I was as helpless as a newborn baby. I checked the window one more time, then hurried to the leather case. Opening it was easy enough. Moving a bag of food and packages of medicine, bandages, a small paper with needle and thread, and a small scissors out of the way, I dug past some carefully folded clothing to papers below. First I came to the map, folded in eighths, then to prescriptions from the infirmary made out for Hans Weiss and Hella Weiss. Next to them were Sarah's keys. He had promised to return them, and I felt a momentary stab of guilt for ever having taken them.

On the spur of the moment, I decided to keep the prescription with my name on it. *He'll be angry about my taking my passport, anyway,* I reasoned, and the prescription was part of my still-unformed plan for independence.

I found the document I had been given at the D.P. camp tied with string to another passport. The second passport

80

was in the name of Kurt Ritter, as was a Persil document, the paper that declared that the person named had never been a Nazi. A German boy from Landsberg once mentioned to Margot and me that these documents were being sold for small fortunes.

I next came across a paper yellow with age, and I unfolded it carefully. I recognized that it was a diploma like the one Maria Burger had on the wall of her apartment. Only this one was from a medical school in Berlin. It was dated 1927, and made out to Kurt Ritter.

*Now that's odd,* I thought, refolding the paper. *Why would my father have Kurt Ritter's diploma?*

Underneath were many packs of Camels cigarettes, too many to stop and count, a packet of German money, a bottle of ink and a pen. There was also a cloth bag filled with coins. Opening it carefully, I took out the one on top, a gold Dutch coin, then returned it to the bag.

Another cloth package was of an irregular shape. Feeling through the covering, I could make out a ring. Perhaps the ring could help answer some of the questions in my mind, but before I began unwrapping it, I heard footsteps on the stairs. Replacing everything but the two papers with my name on them, I shut the top of the satchel without fastening it and dove into my cot just as the door opened.

My eyes shut, I pretended to be sleeping, but I could smell liquor and hear him stumbling about. Cautiously, I opened my eyes a slit, just as my father pulled off his raincoat and fell sprawling on the bed, his shoes still on. He immediately began to snore heavily.

*I'm lucky he's drunk,* I thought, rising to return to the satchel to fasten it. As I passed his bed, I noticed that his precious raincoat, which he usually held as closely as his satchel, was hanging over the side, its bottom seemingly weighed down and full of irregular bumps. Since he was snoring regularly now, I was brave enough to feel the hem of his coat. Sure enough, I felt things as round and hard as pebbles within the hem.

In Landsberg, I had heard many stories of refugees who had survived the war by selling off the coins and gems they had hidden in their clothing. I had seen with my own eyes the fortune he carried in cigarettes and gold. Even if he used it for the rescue work he did, I resented the way he begrudged me a sardine, and, I recalled in a flash of anger, the way he refused a piece of cheese to a starving traveler.

I was curious to see if there were gems in the hem of his coat. Since he was snoring evenly, I pulled the coat from the bed to the satchel. I would have to cut a few stitches, but I recalled seeing a needle and thread as I searched his bag before, and with them and the scissors, I would be able to cut and resew the hem.

Snipping a few tiny stitches as quickly as I could, I opened a small section of the hem and poured out some of the stones into my cupped hand. A diamond sparkled in my palm and a ruby. Another of the gems was green. I knew the name of that jewel, I thought as some deep memory stirred within me. *Emerald. That's the name.*

Suddenly, faintly, I remembered my mother singing about green eyes. "Green eyes like yours, Hella."

*That was right. I had green eyes. But she and Ruth did not. Only I and my father. That was the memory I was seeking.*

My mother's voice with a laugh just below the surface. "You and your father with your emerald eyes."

The man on the bed snored loudly and turned over. His eyes were closed, but I could picture those sharp little circles

82

of blue. *He is not my father,* I realized with a shudder. *Then who is he, and what does he want with me?*

## CHAPTER EIGHT

# Escape Into Danger

For a few moments, I sat paralyzed with the knowledge of my discovery. One thing I was sure of. I didn't want to travel with him, and I had reason enough to leave him. *What a cruel hoax!* I thought bitterly.

Why didn't he realize that as long as he was on a mission rescuing Jews and bringing them to Palestine, I would help him gladly, without his lies, whoever he was. Even now, I would do nothing to harm him. I recalled the young man from B'richa who had stopped off at Landsberg to speak to an assembly of people there. He told us that no one in rescue work kept the money or the possessions for himself—or herself, for there were Jewish women leaders, too, as brave and as strong as the men. I certainly neither needed nor wanted his jewels nor his gold!

But the man sleeping on the bed made me uneasy, and my hand trembled as I tried to thread the needle to resew the lining of the coat. Finally, I was successful, but as I sewed, he stirred. Opening his eyes, he stared straight at me.

I froze with fear. Waiting for his reaction, my breath seemed trapped in my throat. But his vision must have been blurred, for he merely turned over and continued snoring.

After I was finished sewing, I returned the needle to the satchel and took out his military map. I saw we were almost at the border, so close to Merano that I couldn't think of turning back. Of course, if I missed Jack and Norbert and found no one at all to help me, I would have to return to my friends in Landsberg, no matter how long and hard the trip.

My stomach grumbled with hunger, reminding me that I needed food for my journey and something extra for barter. Although Merano looked close enough on a map, the way was through the Alps, and who knew how long it would take? I quietly lifted out several pieces of bread and two packs of cigarettes. I knew it was stealing, but it was the very least I needed to live. Someday I would pay the organization back.

After hiding the bread and cigarettes in my own valise, I lay down on the cot and closed my eyes, thinking of Mama, trying to recall the softness and warmth of her body as she rocked me on her lap.

"You will be strong."

Yes, she had said those very words. Whether it was an order or a prediction, I couldn't recall, but she had said it. I could almost hear her.

I dozed off, and did not awaken until the early morning light. Luckily, the man on the bed, Kurt Ritter, I guessed was his name, was still asleep. Fleeing out of the room and down the steps, I was as quick and as quiet as I could be. I ran into the chilly morning and looked around. Only two people were near, a young woman sweeping the sidewalk in front of her house, as a small child crouched on the ground near her. For a moment, the woman stopped long enough to brush a long stick-like strand of brown hair from her face.

I asked her the way to the Pass, and she pointed it out for me. Thanking her, I hurried on, my shoes the loudest noise on the street. After awhile, I took out a piece of bread and started eating it as I walked. As I was swallowing the last bit, I came to an odd sight which I could not quite make out from a distance. When I came closer, I realized that several people were sleeping huddled under a ragged blanket.

The side of the blanket rippled, and a skinny girl of about nine popped out.

"Do you have any bread for me?" she asked in Polish.

"Who's with you?" I wanted to know, in Yiddish.

Without missing a beat, she, too, spoke Yiddish. "There are three of us, and we haven't eaten a thing since yesterday morning."

"What are you doing here?"

"We were on our way to Bari to get a boat to the Holy Land, but the guards stopped us from leaving Austria."

The mother now pulled the blanket from her face and peered at me. At her side was a smaller child, about six, huddled against her. The two children were dark, with faces as oval as eggs. The woman was light-complected and had a round peasant's face.

"Is this your mother?" I blurted out, for the woman did not look at all like the children.

"She's our mother now," answered the girl. "Our parents left us with her, and she hid us. We are going to the Holy Land now. Do you have any bread?"

How could I refuse? I opened my suitcase and gave her one of the two remaining pieces. It was so little for the three of them that I opened a pack of cigarettes and handed two of the cigarettes to the girl to use in trade. As the little boy watched with wide eyes, the girl and the woman thanked me again and again, their mouths full of bread.

"Where are you going now?" I asked them.

"Innsbruck," the girl replied. "We are joining a group there, and we'll try to cross the border with them." After a moment's hesitation, she added, "If you have trouble, you can go to Innsbruck, too. Aliyah Bet will help you."

Picking up my suitcase, I thanked her. She walked along with me for a short way crying "Shalom!" as we were about to part.

"Shalom!" I answered, with a surge of emotion. I wondered if we would say "Shalom" in greeting someday. Putting down my suitcase, I hugged her goodbye.

By this time, there were others on both sides of the road, most of them dressed in rags and marching silently, a parade of the miserable. Some pushed handmade carts filled with their sad belongings, more rags and broken furniture. Once in a while, a horse-drawn cart passed, and sometimes a jeep or a truck filled with soldiers.

*Ahead there are the guards from the French, British and American forces, and any of them can stop me and send me back,* I thought with a shudder.

*I have to pretend I must get to the sanitarium,* I told myself, coughing into my hand for practice. If anyone questioned me, I would have to convince him I was sick and needed treatment.

When I looked about from the relatively flat stretch of road, the mountains all around seemed unreal. *Oh, they're real enough,* I thought, shivering from the cold mountain air. They seemed to be of every color—there gray, there rose-colored in the rising sun, there sparkling white.

Patches of snow crackled under my shoes. *What would happen in a snowstorm? I could be blown off the road and down the side of the mountain, and no one would ever see me again, not even my best friends.* As I pictured Margot searching for me in Palestine, perhaps even thinking that I had forgotten her, abandoning our dreams, tears filled my eyes.

*No.* Deliberately I stopped daydreaming. *How impractical to daydream when I have so many difficulties still before me, beginning with my running away from Kurt. Will he be angry? Which will he miss more? Me or the cigarettes?*

The thought made me laugh out loud, and an Italian woman refugee turned to look at me, obviously surprised by the sound of laughter. The woman traveled with a child about four, a rope around the child's waist tied to her mother's wrist.

"Bongiorno," she greeted me, taking her eyes off the child only momentarily.

Imitating her, I replied "Bongiorno."

As she continued speaking, all I could understand were the words for French and Italian guards. When she saw I did not speak Italian, she pointed to where other refugees were lining up, rubbed two fingers together, and rolled her eyes to let me know that the guards sought bribes. Nodding, I tried to show her I understood.

Instead of getting in line, the little girl tried to run ahead, but her mother brought her back with a sharp tug which induced loud wails, followed by a slap to the girl's face, and even louder wails. While she hung back to scold her daughter, I went to join the line, opening my suitcase as I stood there and slipping out my papers and the two packs of cigarettes, sticking each pack into a pocket.

Recalling my excuse for entering Italy, I coughed again. In the chilly air, with my legs sore and the soles of my feet burning, I could easily convince myself, at least, that I was not well. *I have to look sick, too,* I thought, letting my shoulders slump.

When I handed the French guard my papers, with a cough, he drew back. After glancing at the papers, he raised his eyes to my face. "Where's your French permit?" he asked.

*French permit!* Vaguely I recalled the need for permits when leaving a particular zone. "I...I don't have one," I stammered.

His expression was hard as he handed me back my papers.

I recalled that the French were known for their kindness to children. "I'm only..." I paused. *My age is right there on the identification paper.* "...thirteen," I said. "Please, sir."

Still no change in expression. The cigarettes. I would have to give some up or remain in Austria forever, God forbid. Only I could not bribe him in front of everyone. I noticed a small shack, for bad weather, nearby.

"May I speak to you in the booth, sir?"

Finally, a spark of interest shone in his face. He led me to the shack. Once inside, he asked impatiently, "Well, what is it?"

But I had been momentarily shocked into silence. For there on the floor, in the midst of an odd collection including a bird cage and a hand-embroidered blanket, was a red carpetbag exactly like the one Margot had offered me only a couple of nights before. *Am I going mad—seeing Margot's possessions everywhere I turn?*

"Well?"

I had to tear my eyes from the bag to answer the guard. Thrusting the open pack of cigarettes at him, I cried, "Please, sir, take it."

Studying the pack, he seemed to be deciding if it were enough. *I should have given him the closed pack,* I thought with regret, wondering if I would have to give that one up, too. Then he barked at me, "All right. Go."

89

I turned quickly before he changed his mind. I couldn't risk another moment there, not even to investigate the red carpetbag.

Further down on the road, other soldiers, mostly Italian, were walking, and I kept as far out of their path as I could. Around noon, I rested on a large gray rock at the side of the road, but I was afraid to nap. As much as the regular army of the occupation frightened me, so did the ragged soldiers returning home from service in Germany or Austria. I guess I was afraid of men in uniforms, *except, of course, Sergeant de Fillippi, who was always joking affectionately with us,* I thought, smiling to myself at the pleasant memory.

After eating the last of the bread, I dragged myself up and continued on. Luckily, I was able to hitch a ride on a hay wagon when the Italian woman with the little girl beckoned to me from their seats in the back of the wagon. I rode with them until some Italian guards made the driver stop so they could check all of our papers. Again, I fingered the pack of cigarettes I might have to use as a bribe, but the guard took a look at my prescription to the sanitarium and another look at me, and with a sympathetic expression he waved me on, into his country.

*Thank God,* I thought, waving good-bye to the Italian woman who had befriended me, grabbing my suitcase and practically running down the road with it, before the other guards could stop me. Since Italy was occupied by the British who could still turn me back, I was not out of danger, but I was getting closer to my goal. With the cigarettes still in my pocket, I followed the scent of cooking to the thick wooden door of an inn. Inside, long wooden tables and benches were set up the width of the place, under a ceiling with exposed wooden beams. Most of the customers, I noticed, were Austrian, rather than Italian.

Placing my suitcase under the table where it could lean against my leg, I sat on a bench near a family of Austrians, also traveling, their belongings under the table and spilling into the aisle and on the bench.

I ordered a vegetable stew and was waiting for it, my attention caught by the way the family next to me was dividing their sausages, when a familiar voice behind me whispered in my ear.

"So, you tried to run away."

## CHAPTER NINE

# Trip To The Edge

My heart skipped a beat as I slowly turned to the man who had called himself my father. Sweaty and breathing hard, he was now studying me with the same intensity with which I regarded him.

"Move over," he gasped, taking the space next to me on the bench.

As the waiter put my stew before me, I felt a pang of guilt for having taken the cigarettes that had paid for my meal. "Would you like some?" I asked the man next to me, as a way of apologizing.

His answer was a look of utter disdain before ordering a beer from the waiter.

*He's not any better than before*, I thought. I knew he would resent my eating in front of him, but too bad for him. I was hungry.

I was popping the stew into my mouth, relishing the taste, when I decided to find out his real name, or at least the alias he was using. "Kurt?" I asked.

Choking on the beer he was swigging, he banged the stein down on the crude table and looked around. Then he narrowed his eyes and leaned menacingly close to me. "You are coming out of here with me," he said.

"Why?" I asked him, moaning the word. *What in the world does he want with me?* I couldn't imagine why he would ever want to see me again. As for me, I would never forgive him for his deception.

The boy from B'richa had told us that some of our people found it easier to evade border guards by traveling in "families" rather than alone. *I would have gladly helped our cause, even if the man I accompanied was not my father. I would have happily pretended to be his daughter. Besides, we had already crossed into Italy, so why does he have to hound me?*

"I am not your daughter. You don't like me. Why can't we go our separate ways?"

His breathing was more labored, and he grimaced with pain, grabbing his arm below the burn. At that moment, I couldn't help feeling sorry for him and decided to lighten his mood.

"You remind me of a story that was going around about acting suspiciously, you know?" Lapsing into Yiddish, I related the story of the wise rabbi who sought a thief among his congregation. "He gathered all his people into the synagogue, then shouted, 'The thief's hat is burning!' The man who raised his hand to his head was the guilty one."

When I finished, I waited for his reaction, but his only response was the familiar look of contempt. His beer had made an ugly white line over his lip. Now he banged the stein on the table. "What are you jabbering about?" he muttered. "Speak German!"

One of the vegetables in the stew caught in my throat. I suddenly couldn't swallow, from the shock of realizing something that should have been obvious from the start. *He used German because he doesn't speak Yiddish. Is he even Jewish? And if he isn't Jewish, why is he risking his life for Jews? Why is he going to Palestine?* It seemed that everything he had told me was a lie.

"Why are you looking at me like that?"

Although it was warm in the restaurant, I felt chilled. "Who are you? Who is Kurt Ritter?"

"Shut up!" He glanced around, as though fearful of my being overheard, then he returned his ice blue eyes to my face. "Don't say that name again."

So many pieces seemed to be in the puzzle, and I still couldn't make out any pattern.

Thinking out loud, I began, "You must have been in a concentration camp, since you had a tattoo on your arm..."

"You think I was tattooed with numbers? You saw a tattoo with numbers on my arm?" Now he was scoffing at me. "Did you ever actually see that, clever girl?"

*He's right. I only assumed that the burn had obliterated his tattoo.*

But there was something else. "You knew my father, didn't you? You knew about Ruth."

Now he sat back, looking as smug as the fat farmers during food rationing. He was in control and sure of himself as I waited breathlessly for his explanation.

"Your father was in Auschwitz. And I was in Auschwitz. Your father was a doctor. And I was a doctor. But your father worked for me. Understand? He took orders from me."

Everything he said both revolted and frightened me, but he did know my father long after I had heard any news of him. "Was my father...?" My voice faltered. "Is he...?"

He knew what I was asking him, and his expression was one of gloating as he replied. "You'll never see him on this earth again. It was close to the end of the war. He and his gang stole weapons and tried to escape. But he was caught." He took a swig of his beer. "I saw his body."

My mind reeled with the news, the scene swaying and blurring before me. Yet some instinct warned me to accept what he said without thinking. *To dwell on my father's death would paralyze me, and I can't afford the luxury of mourning him, not now.*

"Get up!" he demanded, standing over me, like a wall between me and the rest of my life.

I held on to the table as I rose, still weak from his words, and glanced over the crowded benches. *Is there anyone in this whole place who will come to my aid?*

There were no soldiers of the occupation forces around, no French or American or British, not even any of the local police. And I could not rely on the Austrian burghers or the few Italians with their families to help me. Still, I was safer here in the restaurant with so many people than outside alone with Ritter.

With only one weapon, I needed strength to use it. At that moment, my mother's voice echoed in my mind. "Be strong. You must save yourself—for me."

*Yes, Mama,* I vowed. *I will save myself for your sake.*

"I am not going with you, Kurt Ritter," I shouted at the top of my voice. Other noises in the place quieted as the people turned to see what was going on. "You belong in Nuremburg with the other Nazis. Kurt Ritter!" I shouted his name again and again. Every time I used it, he flinched as though I had hit him.

A man shouted, "Enough! Can't you let me eat in peace!" and Ritter jerked his head to see where the voice came from. When he saw everyone in the place staring at us, his eyes widened, his nostrils twitched, and he stumbled into the aisle as I shouted after him, "Don't come back. Everyone knows your name, Kurt Ritter. Everyone knows who you are! Nazi!"

Without looking back, he made his way to the door. By the time he reached it, the people in the restaurant were returning to their own private conversations. My knees, I realized, felt the consistency of cooked noodles, and I sank back on the bench where I had been sitting.

No one came to me. No one cared to help me as I sat there alone and more hopeless than ever. Outside, Ritter was hiding, waiting for me, no doubt, the silly child who walked, no, willingly ran, into his snare. He must have planned all along to kill me when he reached his destination. Now there was no escape.

A narrow rivulet of beer flowed on the table in front of me. One of the boys in the family at the table had spilled his father's beer while reaching for a piece of sausage, and his father was smacking him on the head as the boy tried to move out of his range. The boy looked younger than me, but he was my size. As he put out his hand to pick up the mug that had toppled, I noticed the sleeve of a woolen undershirt at his wrist and the ragged sleeve of a rough shirt over that. His coat lay on the floor, and on his straight blonde hair he wore a cap.

*Can it work?* I wondered.

I slid closer to the family. The father stopped hitting his son long enough to glance my way.

"You heard me with that man who was here, the Nazi?"

As the father curled his lip in disdain, I feared it was for me, not Kurt. *No matter. I can't lose my nerve now,* I thought. "If I could borrow your son's cap and jacket...just till I get to the woods."

"He needs them," the man growled, turning away with a raised hand for his son.

"I can pay you."

That won his attention.

His wife's eyes widened as she eagerly sat forward. "What do you have?"

I quickly calculated what I needed till Merano, still a hard thirty-five kilometers away. "Half a pack of cigarettes," I answered.

Her eyes narrowed, "That's not enough."

She caught me by surprise. I tried to think out what to offer next, but all the emotions I had just experienced, plus my terror at the danger I still faced, combined like different currents of air to fog my mind. In a panic, I took the whole pack out of my pocket and thrust it at the woman.

"Here. Is this enough?"

Leaning over, she grabbed the pack from my hand, turning it this way and that in her beefy hands, as though I had planned to spring a trick on her. Glancing at me, she opened it, studied the contents, then held it to her nose to sniff. When she was satisfied, she nodded to her husband.

Still breathless with fear, I told her my plan. "Ritter is probably waiting outside, but if I put on your son's things and we walk together in a group, he won't recognize me."

The woman agreed.

I put out my hand for the pack, which she was reluctant to give up, and emptied about half onto the table. "I'll give you the rest when I'm safe."

Her eyes sparkled with greed as she put the cigarettes in the sack she carried. *Thank goodness she could not guess what Ritter was hiding in his satchel and his coat or I would be lost,* I thought.

I exchanged my jacket for the boy's coat, which was longer and heavier than I thought, and stuck my hair under the filthy cap he gave me. I saw I needed his boots, too, to shove the bottom of my skirt into, but that was not part of the bargain, his mother reminded me.

"Please," I begged her. "You can see my skirt under the coat."

But she remained tight-lipped and stubborn. Finally, I pulled out a blouse from my suitcase for her. Now she was satisfied, directing her son to let me exchange his boots temporarily for my shoes.

The boots flapped beyond my toes, and the boy complained that my shoes pinched his feet. "They're girls' shoes," he added with a whine, but a smack from his father quieted him.

I lifted my suitcase. By now, I had learned to speak more forcefully. "Hide this with your bundles."

The mother directed the boy to cover the valise with his bundles. Then, organizing our exit at the door, she placed me in the middle of her two sons, with her husband and herself on the far outside.

As we walked out, I kept my head down, fighting an urge to look around. Meanwhile, "mother" was keeping up a steady stream of chatter. I knew she was speaking about food, but the words had lost their meaning for me.

When we came to the edge of the town, she stopped. "You're clear now."

It took all my courage, but I insisted they go further with me. "To the road. To where others are walking," I told them, gesturing ahead where travelers were wending their way, and we continued on.

Before exchanging the boy's clothing with him, I peered all around, but Ritter was nowhere in sight. I struck a last bargain with the mother, keeping her son's dirty cap in exchange for a fairly new kerchief given to me recently at Landsberg. I figured that at a distance, the cap would be the better disguise.

My jacket was nowhere near as warm as the coat I had given back, and the weather was getting colder. *If it snows, I'll freeze,* I thought with a shudder, for I had no really warm clothing and no boots, and already I couldn't feel my feet. What's more, my bread was gone, and I had only a few possessions to trade.

My heart fell, for what was the use anyway? *My father is dead, just like my darling mother and my sister and Herman and...and. Is there any end to my loss?*

I thought of Mama. *I'm trying,* I said to her. *I won't forget what you told me, but, forgive me, you told Ruth the same thing, and what good did it do her?*

As the dark storm clouds raced overhead, I felt ashamed of my thoughts. The oncoming storm made me think of another night, not long ago. On our way to Berlin, Margot and I had found shelter in an abandoned garage. I fell asleep, but thunder awakened me during the night. When I glanced at Margot, she was lying with her eyes wide open.

"What are you doing?" I had asked her.

"Praying," she answered.

"What are you praying for?"

For a moment, she hesitated. Then she told me. "I would like to close my eyes, fall asleep and never awaken again."

"No. Don't say that," I cried, holding my arms out to her, seeking words to banish her despair. "What would I do without you?"

*What will Margot do without me? What will Palestine do without all of us, all the orphans?*

99

*One foot after another,* I told myself. My legs ached and I could not feel my toes. My suitcase was becoming heavier and heavier. *One foot after another.*

I had to go on. I had to imagine I was in Palestine carrying water that would irrigate the dry earth. Arab neighbors working alongside us were helping us cultivate lush fruits and vegetables. Although my body strained almost unbearably with the weight, I would not stop....

Missing a sudden descent, I fell forward on a rock, gashing my knee. That made me sob out loud, and my sob echoed through the mountains.

Dark was coming swiftly—or was it the dark before a storm? I couldn't tell. Far in the distance were some lights and a structure. *Probably a farmhouse. I'll have to make my way to it,* I told myself, imaging it as a besieged farm in Palestine. *I am the only hope for all my friends from our kibbutz in Landsberg. Margot, Esther, Olga, Jack, Norbert...who all depend on me to get through.* I labored on with my knee stinging and stiffening and my legs as heavy as the boulders all around me.

By the time I reached the road to the farmhouse, it was dark, and huge snowflakes were falling. My legs were two pains below a stomach aching with hunger. The light in the farmhouse was a beacon which I had to reach, no matter what.

It was farther than I thought. As I came closer, the ground became covered with a thin white sheet on which my shoes made black impressions. As I hobbled down the path to the house, I noticed a truck near it, a covered army truck, on which were written words in English. Even with the snow gathering on the cover, I could tell the truck was British.

I could not help groaning out loud. *Have I walked out of my way to a farmhouse filled with British soldiers? The British,* I thought bitterly, for the words reminded me of the ships full of refugees they had sent back from Palestine to their certain deaths in Europe during the war. *Even now they deny the Saved Remnant their homeland.*

As I stood there, unable to decide where to hide or what to do, another truck, its headlights like the eyes of some monster hurtling through the snow, turned onto the field next to the farmhouse. Unable to move, partly from exhaustion, partly from fear, I stood like a statue until a soldier leaned his head out of the window and called something out to me in English. When I didn't respond, he tried Italian.

I turned to run away, darting towards the back of the house, but I was no match for the soldier. He caught me and tackled me to the ground. *It's all over,* I thought. *Now I'm really in trouble.*

## CHAPTER TEN

# Steep And Treacherous

When he rose, he addressed me again in Italian. I didn't understand his words, but I did understand the gesture he made towards the house.

"Please, I dropped my valise on the ground," I told him in German. "May I get it?"

"German?" he asked.

For a moment, I wondered if I should tell him I was Jewish. Then he might guess my destination and try to send me back to Germany. Besides, if he asked to see my papers, he would be able to figure everything out soon enough. *It is better not to say anything*, I decided.

I answered with a brief "Yes."

With his hand on my arm, he led me back to the suitcase and then to the farmhhouse.

A young woman greeted him at the door, questioning him about me in English. From the few words I caught, I guessed she was asking him where I was headed. We both followed her into the living room, a big place with blankets all around and some civilians of various ages around a blazing fireplace. A couple of the people turned their attention to me, and my first thought was that they were Jewish. *Perhaps they, too, were caught by the British while trying to get to the Holy Land.* But before I could think any more about it, the woman began questioning me in German with a heavy Polish accent.

"What are you doing here?" she asked.

"I'm going to the sanitarium at Merano." Recalling my alleged reason for going there, I coughed.

"Where are you from?"

My papers had been issued at Landsberg. There was no point in lying when they could discover the truth so easily.

I told her, and, without skipping a beat, she asked, "From the D.P. camp?"

To admit being from the camp was to admit being Jewish, and from that, the woman might start questioning me about my going to Palestine. *I will insist that I am going to the sanitarium,* I thought.

"Well," the woman said impatiently. "Are you from the camp or not?"

Glancing at the people around the fire, who now were listening to my questioning with interest, I felt my weariness like the bundles I had carried on my back on the farm. I wanted so to belong, to join those resting in the warmth of the fireplace, no matter the consequences.

"Yes, I'm from the camp at Landsberg."

"You're Jewish?"

Lifting my chin, I met her steady blue eyes. "Yes, I'm Jewish."

For some odd reason, that seemed to amuse her. She broke into a grin, then in Yiddish to everyone in the room. "You hear that? The girl's Jewish!"

The soldier who had tackled me outside now slapped my shoulder, laughing gleefully. A woman sitting in the glow of the fire rose to hug me. Confused by their reactions, I stood there stiffly.

"Look at the soldier's insignia," directed the woman, in Yiddish now, with a Polish accent.

103

Turning to the soldier, I focused on his shoulder, and I, too, smiled. I was looking at a Jewish Star!

The Polish woman took me around by the waist. "He fought in the British Army with other Palestinian Jews. This house you stumbled upon is a secret station for our people going to southern Italy and from there to Palestine. I am Rifka, and I welcome you for all of us!"

They crowded around me now, asking me how I had come from Landsberg. Thankfully, Dalia, the woman who had originally questioned me, insisted on feeding me, so I told my story sitting in the kitchen, between bites of pasta and tangy cheese and gulps of hot tea.

"The Alps are crawling with Nazis," remarked the soldier. "They're on their way to Spain and Portugal and southern Italy, but we can't do our work and chase them, too."

"They're all through Italy. Some of them use the same routes we do and stay at the same stations. We're leaving here for Merano later tonight," added Rifka, the Polish woman.

"Merano! That's where I was headed!" I blurted out. "I'm hoping to meet some friends from Landsberg there."

"We have a truckload tonight," said the soldier.

I could not hide my disappointment, and he noticed it.

"But we can always use one more." Glancing outside at the falling snow, he joked, "We can use your added weight so we won't fall off the mountain."

I stood at the window with him, watching the flakes dotting the light. "Isn't it dangerous?" I asked.

"We make the trip in all kinds of weather. What might be bad for traveling is good for evading the British," he reassured me.

Since we weren't leaving until later, I fell asleep on the only spot available, the floor near the fireplace. In the midst of a deep, dreamless sleep, I was shaken awake and told to get ready to leave. Dalia had a pot of strong coffee to help us stay alert. With the others, I drank the bitter brew.

The snow had stopped falling, and the air was crisp and clear now. A sparkling white blanket lay on the ground like some wizard's beguiling gift.

We must have been ten people climbing into the truck. Rifka gestured to me to sit next to her, and I did. Huddling together from lack of space and for warmth made me think of the comfort of friends. But the more I thought of Jack and Norbert, the more worries disturbed me. *What if I don't find them? Then what? The others in the truck know where they are going and when. I don't even know my friends' plans past Merano. I can easily miss them....* I sighed aloud. Rifka glanced at me, noticed my creased forehead, and put an arm around my shoulder.

"What's the matter?" she asked so sympathetically that I spilled my concerns right out, all over her.

When I finished, she replied, "Who's safe? What's certain? You've come this far," she reminded me, "and you'll always find other Jews who will help you."

Feeling comforted, I rested my head against her shoulder. The truck bounced along under a ceiling of bright stars above us. Once, the tires slipped, and we gasped collectively, for we traveled along the edge of a narrow road, and between our path and the valley below was eternity.

Eventually, I nodded off. When I awoke, the covering I had seen before on the truck was over our heads. Peeking from under it, I saw we were in a town. Then, as in a dream, I saw a sight that elated me. We were approaching a chalet, lit by the moon and a lamppost next to its front

105

door.  It was exactly like the one I had pictured all along! How quaint it was, with its balconies of carved wood and its low sloping roof edged with huge timbers.  That was the place, I was sure, for how else could I have pictured it so accurately?  Unfortunately, the soldiers drove past it, kept driving, and finally stopped at a large decrepit inn about a half-mile away.

They opened the cover above us, then gestured that we should be still.  I wanted to glance again in the direction of the chalet, but we had to hurry along without attracting attention, and so I quickly followed Rifka who was directly in front of me.  Once inside, while our leader, a gray-haired man, was talking with the concierge, I stood as taut as an animal ready to pounce, for I knew I had to make my move to the chalet before the group I was with went to its sleeping quarters.

Turning to Rifka, I whispered, "Don't worry about me. I think I saw where my friends are.  Shalom."

She leaned towards me, as though on the verge of detaining me, but the others were moving forward now and I was already turned in the direction of the door.  Before she could even answer "Shalom," I was on my way out.

As I made my way down the quiet road, I smiled with the joyful thought of meeting with Jack and Norbert.  I could hear myself describe the intuition that led me to them.  My daydreams were so pleasant that before I knew it, I was in front of the chalet.

After pushing open the wooden door, I found myself in a lobby I could have pictured, too.  Great planks made up most of the walls and a mammoth stone fireplace, with embers now glowing on black logs, faced the doorway.

No one was at the desk, so I considered simply walking up the staircase and calling Jack and Norbert's names at

106

every landing, but before I could get to the stairs, I heard a door open and a harsh voice shouting in German, "Stop! Where are you going?"

A slight man wearing thick spectacles was watching me as intently as if I had invaded his home with a rifle under my arm.

"I believe my friends are...may be here. They are from Landsberg. Two boys..."

It was a simple enough query, but he snarled and spat an answer. "I know of no such people. What would they do here? Where were you sneaking to?"

At that moment, from a room at the side of the lobby I had not noticed, a man emerged, ducking his head at the doorway. No, not a man, a giant! Even his close-cropped head seemed mythic.

"Get out!" the smaller man with spectacles ordered me. "Don't you come back, either. Throw her out!" he ordered the giant who, I guessed, must have been a guard or a bouncer.

Although I didn't know why I was being treated that way, I didn't choose to argue. I ran to the front door, an eye on the giant stepping in my direction. Once outside, I gladly gulped down the clear, fresh air.

*Who are they?* I thought, watching the door, quite sure now that the men would return to their rooms without coming to look any farther for me. *Why did they treat me so shabbily? I only wanted to ask a simple question.*

That reminded me of my friends. Searching the tiny windows, most of them dark, I decided that I couldn't call Jack and Norbert by name and risk getting them into trouble. But I could try to let them know that I was there. If they heard me, they would find a way to answer.

"Friends," I shouted at the chalet, "It's Hella. Hella is here. Hella is calling her friends."

"Shut up. Go away. Shut up," a man in a nightshirt called from his balcony.

"It's Hella!"

A light went on. A woman's voice called out from another room, "Are you crazy? Do you know the hour? You crazy!" I strained to understand her accented German.

The front door squeaked open, and the giant man I had seen before was walking menacingly to me. His clenched fists reminded me of the boulders that bounced down mountains in avalanches.

"Oh, no!" I moaned, turning and running back in the direction of the inn I had come from. With no clear thought in mind, I ran until my aching legs and straining lungs made me stop. When I looked behind me, the road was empty.

Suddenly, I realized why I had been able to run so swiftly. I had left my valise behind somewhere. I tried to remember when I had it last. *On the road,* I recalled, *right in front of the chalet. I must have put it down while I was shouting at the windows.*

All my possessions—except the clothing I was wearing and the precious identification paper I kept in my pocket— were in that valise—all my other clothes, even the music box. *Oh, that music box. What memories it stirred. How could I have lost it?*

I would have to go back, as much as I hated the thought. This time, I walked close to the buildings, hopefully in the shadows. No one else was out at this hour, in this remote village, and the middle of the road outside the chalet was absolutely empty. No car. No cart. No valise.

The giant with the shorn head had seen me drop it and run. He was the most likely thief, but what would he want with my few items of wear? And the thought of him listening to the tinkle of "The Blue Danube" on a music box was so ridiculous I would laugh, if I weren't so close to tears.

Although the very last thing I cared to do was go inside the chalet again, I had no choice. I had to get my things back.

The squeak of the front door brought both the concierge and his bodyguard out of their rooms.

"My v-valise," I stammered. "I need my..."

"What valise?" sneered the concierge. He pointed to the door. "Out of here, fast, or I will call the police, do you hear?"

The bodyguard stepped forward, arms folded, like some supernatural being in a fable. His eyes drilled into mine, and suddenly I realized the danger I was in. They were not returning my valise, for whatever reason. That was certain.

For the second time that night, I turned and bolted out of the chalet. As I stepped outside, I awkwardly tripped over a stone sticking out of the stone walk. Looking down, I saw it wasn't part of the walk at all. It was my valise, which I grabbed in one quick motion. Running as swiftly as I could, I made my way back to the hotel and Rifka and the others.

I entered the lobby breathlessly, and weary from the long, long night, dragged myself towards the concierge's desk. Vaguely, I sensed someone approaching me from the side. I turned my head to look, then stopped dead in my tracks.

Limping straight towards me, a hand in his gun pocket and breathing heavily, was Kurt Ritter!

## CHAPTER ELEVEN

# My Friend's Gun

My choices flashed before me. *I can't run out, for then I will be in greater danger. He's too strong for me to fight, and, of course, there's that gun in his pocket. Shouting worked before...*

"No! Kurt Ritter. Nazi. Nazi Ritter. Help me, someone! Help me!"

From the corner of my eye, I saw a husky blond man and the concierge behind the desk watching me without any visible emotion. But some of the people standing around turned to me, and the gray-haired man, who had led Rifka and the rest of us from the farmhouse, now was rushing towards Ritter. I was aware, also, of the sound of feet trampling down the staircase.

A gun went off, the noise engulfing me. I felt a pressure in my chest. Gulping for air, I tried to scream, but I couldn't hear my scream, only its echo. As I fell to the floor, I thought, *He shot me.*

But when I came to, I felt no sharp pain anywhere. I raised a hand to touch my chest. No blood, no wound. Nothing but the rough wool of my jacket.

"You're all right, darling."

The voice was Margot's. I looked up to see my shirt hovering over me, but, *no, it isn't my shirt anymore,* I recalled. *I gave it to Margot. Is this another dream?*

She responded as if she had read my mind. "Yes, I'm really here. And so are Jack and Norbert."

110

Jack, too, kneeled next to me, his finger nervously rubbing the scar on his cheek. "You're not hurt, Hella. You can get up. And Ritter is gone," he said. "I fired a shot in the air and that sent him scurrying."

Again, I lifted my eyes to Margot, and again she knew what I wanted to know.

"After you left Landsberg, some American MP's came looking for a Kurt Ritter. He was a Nazi whose own people turned him in for killing a woman who was supposed to help him escape to Spain," she explained.

Jack added, "He thought that traveling with you as your father would help him pass more easily. He probably planned to kill you when he didn't need you anymore."

Jack was right, and the thought chilled me.

Seeing me shivering, Margot hugged me. "We had to warn you and rescue you from him. Sergeant de Fillippi himself drove me all the way to the Brenner Pass. But when we couldn't find you, he had to turn back."

I recalled the red carpetbag I had seen in the little guardhouse. "Your carpetbag?" I asked.

She knew what I meant. "Yes," she murmured, nodding. "I had to leave it because the French guards wouldn't let me through unless I showed I would return to Germany. But I never saw you or Ritter anywhere on the road. That cap you're wearing might have thrown me off."

I explained how I got the cap. That reminded me. "What happened with Ritter?" I asked Jack. "Can he come back?"

"I hope we scared him off, Hella, but there's nothing more we can do, unless we get him alone outside. That's another story. But we can't jeopardize our use of the inn

111

by going after him here. Another group, one from Yugoslavia, is meeting us here tonight."

Rifka and the gray-haired man came over to see how I was. Helped up by Jack and Norbert, holding onto Margot, I let them all, friends old and new, lead me to the staircase, but then I followed the ones from my Landsberg kibbutz.

"We're on the third floor," Jack remarked as we started up the steps. "The whole floor is for our people only."

Turning to Margot, I asked her, "Did you speak to him about our going to Palestine?"

With eyes widening, she shook her head.

"What about Margot and me?" I asked as we slowly climbed up the steps. "We don't want to have to go all the way back to Landsberg. Can we go with you on this trip—to Palestine?"

He pondered my question for a moment. "I wish you could come," he finally answered, "but there are so many waiting, Hella, and we still don't know how many the ship will hold."

Stopping on a landing, I sighed in disappointment.

"If you can't make it this trip, there are camps in Italy where you can study agriculture and Hebrew until the next ship."

"Or the next," Margot said.

Reluctantly, Jack agreed. "There's no telling when there'll be ships for everyone."

"Italy's closer to Palestine than Landsberg," Margot murmured to me. "At least we'll be ready when they're ready for us."

When we reached the third floor, I was surprised to see an attractive young woman with bright lipstick sitting on a chair under the single light bulb, guarding the hallway. Margot introduced me to her before leading me to her room, which she shared with other girls and women, two to a bed, some on the floor, one sprawled out and snoring on a chair. I wondered how anyone could sleep with such snoring going on, but as soon as I lay down on the floor, sharing Margot's pillow and blanket, I, too, fell asleep.

Sometime during the night, there were noises in the hall. I opened the door to see Jack leading some new arrivals to another room. Wide awake, I thought I'd never go back to sleep, so as quietly as I could, I began washing in the sink, drying my hands and face on my clothing. When I opened the door again, Jack was sitting guard alone under the light, a gun within reach under his chair.

"Shalom," he greeted me. "You couldn't sleep?"

As I nodded, I felt the shyness I always experienced near a boy I liked.

"Are you tired?" he asked as I stood awkwardly, unable to arrange either my legs or my arms comfortably.

Jack was waiting for an answer.

"I'm not tired," I answered. "What about you? When did you sleep?"

"I slept early, before you came. Margot woke me up when she heard your voice and we both ran downstairs."

"Oh." I had run out of conversation when I noticed a book on his lap. "What are you reading?"

With a smile, he picked the book up to show it to me. It was in Hebrew. "I'm still learning," he said.

He had been one of the assistant teachers in our kibbutz, but everyone knew he kept only a lesson ahead of the rest of us.

113

"Come." After putting out his arm to draw me nearer, he opened the book and held it out for me to read.

I began by stumbling even over the words I knew, for I was too conscious of his presence and his arm around my waist to concentrate.

He looked up. "I have an easier book inside. I'll get it for you." Standing, he gestured to his seat. "You can take my place for a minute."

"You're leaving the gun?" I asked.

"You know how to use it?"

I was surprised at his question, for guns in Germany had been more plentiful than potatoes after the war. On our way to Berlin, Margot and I had found a loaded gun in the fields that we later bartered for soap and towels. But before we traded it away, we took practice shots. "Of course I know how to use a gun," I answered Jack, picking up the gun from under the chair and weighing it in my hand.

"I'll be right back. Don't shoot anyone," Jack warned me jokingly as he disappeared into his room.

A moment after the door closed, I heard a noise in the dark near the steps.

"Who is it?" I asked.

The familiar voice that answered was like the shock of icy water. "You can't see me, can you, Hella? But I can see you fine."

Ritter was right, I couldn't see him, and I was terribly vulnerable. Jumping up from the chair, I pulled the string of the light overhead with my free hand, and leaped from the seat. In total darkness now, I couldn't find my own hand if it weren't attached to my arm.

"Why don't you leave me alone?" I cried in frustration, moving along the wall so he wouldn't find me by the direction of my voice. I was fully aware that with any step, I could bump into him.

"You had to look through my satchel," he answered, from what seemed to be somewhere on the far side of the stairs. "And that wasn't enough for you, so you opened my coat. You know too much."

"You can't harm me. This place is full of my friends."

"My friends, too."

"Not if you shoot me. Didn't you get into trouble once already?"

He didn't answer, and I felt a doorknob at my side. I had stumbled into the knob of the door to Jack's room. What if Ritter started shooting? The thought of Jack's getting hurt because of me, or any of the others for that matter, was too painful. I had to keep moving to find Kurt.

I kept stepping along the wall, the floor creaking beneath my shoes, when Ritter surprised me by announcing, "I'll be back."

The next sounds I heard were his footsteps on the stairs and, a moment later, a door closing on the floor below.

*What now?* I wondered. *If I tell Jack and the others, they might want to fight Ritter, and the plans for Aliyah of scores of people traveling hundred, even thousands of miles might be endangered. It's my fight,* I told myself, *my silly overactive imagination that made me think even for a moment that Ritter was my father.*

*No,* I decided. *I'm not going to risk my friends' safety anymore because of my foolishness. I started this trouble, and I'm going to take care of it.*

A picture of myself in Palestine, rifle in hand, protecting my kibbutz, came into my mind. *Our country is not going to be won or kept by the meek,* I thought, making my way to the staircase and the floor below.

On the second floor, a single naked bulb shone in the center of the hall, just as it did on the floor above. And, again, the illumination from the single light didn't reach into the dark corners or the recessed doors of most of the rooms.

I heard a shout in German behind one of the closed doors. Ritter's voice answered, followed by a thud. Concentrating on reaching the room without being discovered by any of the other escaping Nazis Kurt considered his "friends," I never noticed that someone else was in the hall.

A hand gripped my wrist, and in surprise, my fingers loosened, and the gun I was holding fell.

"What are you doing here?" the man demanded as he crouched to scoop up the gun. When he rose, I saw him in the light and I recognized him at once.

## CHAPTER TWELVE

# Death and New Life

The concierge, who had stood behind the desk when Ritter first confronted me and hadn't moved a muscle to help me, now held the gun that should have been guarding my friends.  Waving it furiously, he berated me, in Italian-accented German, "You can't walk around my hotel with a gun in your hand."

I was going to remind him how he did nothing about Ritter and his gun in the lobby, when we both jumped at the sound of crashing furniture.

"Now what!" exclaimed  the concierge, raising his eyes to the ceiling.

With the gun still trained on me, he tried the door with his other hand.  When it didn't open, he took out a set of keys and fit one into the lock.  The noise of shattering glass in the room distracted him completely from guarding me.  I could have easily escaped as he flung the door open, but I had come to this floor to put an end to the threat of Kurt Ritter for myself and my friends, and, anyway, I wasn't leaving until I got back the gun Jack had trusted me with.

The concierge burst into the room, still holding the gun in front of him, and I followed him in.  He let out a groan at the sight of a chair overturned and broken and a lamp shattered.  The husky blond German I had unsuccessfully appealed to in the lobby was on the floor kneeling over Ritter, banging Ritter's head on the wooden planks, but when he glanced up, he saw the gun in the concierge's hand, he immediately dropped his hold, letting Ritter's head fall with a thud.

117

"He makes trouble," he gasped to the concierge. "He'll bring us all down."

The concierge shook his head. "No one kills in my inn. You want them to close this place? Get up," he ordered the husky blond.

The man stood, while Ritter, groaning and clutching the back of his head, watched him with pure hatred on his face.

"You'll be sorry," the blond warned the concierge while the innkeeper followed him with his eyes and his gun.

"Get out," the concierge replied. "Get out of here."

As the German went to his bags, Kurt Ritter arose dazedly, his arm forming a triangle with his hand on the top of his head, a large circle of blood covering his hair like a skullcap.

I wanted to tell the concierge about Ritter's gun, but before I could, our attention was caught by the gleam of a knife in the husky blond man's hand. As we were watching him and the knife, Ritter dove to a spot near the overturned chair.

"Look out," I shouted when I became aware of what Ritter was doing.

The concierge turned with his gun aimed at Ritter now, but it was too late. Ritter also had a gun in his hand, and he was holding it with a good deal more menace than the concierge.

"Drop it," Ritter told him.

The concierge hesitated.

"My fight isn't with you. They're my enemies," he said, nodding in my direction.

That convinced the concierge. Without another glance at us, he tossed the gun on the bed and fled as quickly out the door as he could.

"Close it," Ritter shouted after him, and the bang of the door closing was as loud as a shot.

"Give me your passport," he directed the husky blonde. Fresh blood had made a red collar all around the back of Ritter's neck.

Keeping his knife out of sight, the blonde man opened his knapsack. Meanwhile, I was closest to the door, and as Ritter kept his eyes on the man, I inched towards it. Accidentally, I kicked the wall with the heel of my shoe, which made a dull thud.

Ritter's head shot around to me, and in that moment, I could read his thoughts: One bullet and he would be rid of me for good.

I ducked low as the sound of gunfire rang through the air. He missed me! I realized that he was distracted from his fight with the blond man. "Get him now," I shouted to the blond. "Stab him."

As Ritter spun around to face him, a gun went off. At that moment, I could have escaped, but I was fascinated by the sight of the two men. Ritter was slumped over the blond while the man was slipping to the floor, carrying Ritter down with him. They looked like drunken dancers.

Before I could approach any closer, there was a bang behind me. I turned just as the door started falling off its hinges—almost on top of me. I jumped out of the way, miraculously unharmed as Jack came running in with other friends right behind him.

"What's going on here, Hella?"

I led them to the two motionless men. The blond was dead from a bullet wound, and when Jack moved Ritter's body, I gasped when I saw the knife deeply imbedded in it right near his heart. The blond had stabbed Ritter when I told him to.

For the second time that night, Jack put an arm around me. "How did this happen?"

I explained to him and to Margot and the others how Ritter had threatened me. "I didn't want anyone else to have to fight him, but, believe me, I was glad you showed up when you did!"

The concierge arrived while I was telling them what happened in the room, and he seemed more upset about the splattered blood than about the two bodies that caused the mess. With a cry and a curse, he ran out again.

"For a good, strong mop," Norbert commented, and we all laughed in relief.

"Let's find our gun," Jack advised his friend.

"What about Ritter's?" Norbert asked him.

"Better leave that for the police to investigate. We don't want anything to hold us up."

"Empty Ritter's satchel," I told them after they had found the gun. Pointing to the blood-soaked raincoat Ritter was wearing, I said, "Take the coat, too."

Jack looked at the garment and back at me, questioningly.

"You won't be sorry, believe me."

When we were back upstairs, everyone placed what they had taken from the satchel on a bed. In addition to everything I had seen before was the ring Jack unwrapped, a ring many recognized as having been worn by members of the Nazis' special police. With Norbert's penknife, I

120

opened the lining of Ritter's coat, pouring gems of every color on the bed. Jack scratched one of the diamonds against the mirror above the sink, and the stone cut the glass.

Only Margot did not join in the general glee. When I asked her why, her explanation sobered us all. "They were probably our gems to begin with."

She was right. The first thing the Nazis had done in every town and city they conquered was to demand the gold and jewelry of the Jews.

Quietly, Jack added, "And now those same diamonds, emeralds and rubies will help get Jews into Palestine where they will make the land flourish. It's not justice, not at all, but it is something."

A knock on the door made us all glance that way. One of the men who had come to the inn after us during the night was standing there. In simple Hebrew, that even I could understand, he asked, "Friends, when do we begin our ascent to Palestine?"

Continuing more easily in Yiddish, he asked Jack, "Did the others you were expecting come?"

"Not all of them," Jack replied. "Some were sent back at the border." He turned to Norbert. "We can't wait any longer. We should be on our way," he announced.

I could sense how anxious everyone felt to continue on their journey southward. Only Margot and I had no definite plans, except finding some other camp for displaced persons. *If I don't speak up now*, I thought, *it might be years before we could make Aliyah. Perhaps we would never make it. To be born and to die on this accursed continent,* I thought, *and never to have any of my family know the joy of our beloved land...*

121

*No, Mama. No, Papa,* I added. *For your sakes as well as mine...*

Repeating Mama's encouragement to myself, I placed myself in front of Jack and motioned to Margot. "What about us?" I asked Jack with a catch in my voice. "Can we come in place of the people who were sent back at the border?"

Jack looked over my head to meet Norbert's eyes. I could tell from the glance that passed between them that they had already discussed my question. "We thought about you, Hella," Jack began. "You know agriculture from the farm you worked on. We could use you in Palestine."

My heart soared. As a reflex, I sought to share my excitement with Margot, but when I turned to her and saw the sadness on her face, I realized that Jack hadn't mentioned her at all.

"What about Margot?"

"Did you ever work on a farm?" Norbert asked her.

Her eyes clouded. "There weren't any gardens where I was," she murmured.

Taking her thin hand in mine, I knew my decision, although unhappy, was right. "It's both of us or neither. I'm not leaving Margot again."

When she started to protest, I interrupted her. "I've made up my mind. I'd rather wait with Margot than go without her."

As I stood there with her hand in mine, I couldn't help thinking of all the others who were waiting. *From one end of Europe to the other, many would never live to see the Promised Land. Some would die on the way, but others would live to thrive there. All were worthy.* And so I

122

wouldn't beg Jack or even say anything else to sway him, not when I thought of all who had to be left behind.

But Jack broke into an encouraging smile. "We thank you for all the treasure you led us to. You've already helped our cause. And Margot is your sister, isn't she?"

Whooping for joy, I flung my arms around Margot, hugging her tight, then pressed the hands Jack and Norbert and the others held out.

Outside, the snow on the ground crunched softly beneath our feet as we walked to the place where trucks would pick us up. Singing softly as we went with our arms looped together, I thought to myself that my daydreams actually were coming true. Although the moment was as perfect as any I dreamed about, I couldn't help imagining myself on a farm in Palestine with my friends working with me in the fields. Now and then, I'd stop to wipe the sweat from my forehead or take a refreshing gulp of water from a canteen passed from hand to hand....

Suddenly, my eye caught the first red line of morning on the horizon. As my heart lifted with the day that was dawning, I stepped forward and thought, *Come, Mama, Papa, my darling Ruth. Come.*